D0970338

Folly's Bride

Also by Jane Peart in Large Print:

Circle of Love
A Distant Dawn
Dreams of a Longing Heart
The Heart's Lonely Secret
Homeward the Seeking Heart
The House of Haunted Dreams
The Pledge
The Promise
The Risk of Loving
Runaway Heart
Shadow of Fear
Thread of Suspicion
Undaunted Spirit
Web of Deception
Where Tomorrow Waits

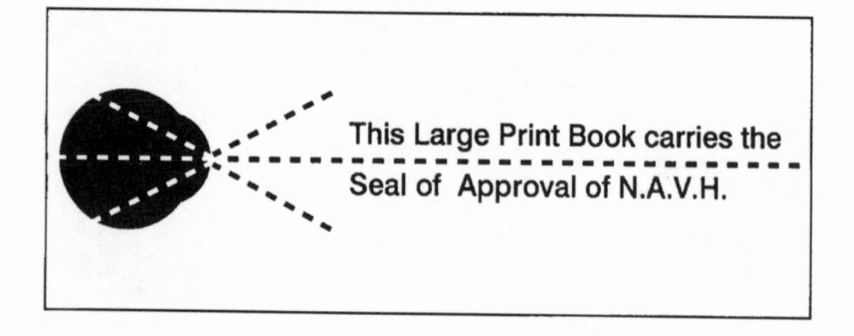

Jane Peart

Book Four
of the Brides of Monclair series

Folly's Bride

Thorndike Press • Waterville, Maine

Published in 2004 by arrangement with
Natasha Kern Literary Agency, Inc.

Thorndike Press® Large Print Christian Romance.

The tree indicium is a trademark of Thorndike Press.

The text of this Large Print edition is unabridged.
Other aspects of the book may vary from the original edition.

Set in 16 pt. Plantin by Al Chase.

Printed in the United States on permanent paper.

Library of Congress Cataloging-in-Publication Data

Peart, Jane.
Folly's bride / Jane Peart.
p. cm. — (Brides of Montclair series ; bk. 4)
ISBN 0-7862-6718-6 (lg. print : hc : alk. paper)
1. Plantation owners' spouses — Fiction. 2. Williamsburg Region (Va.) — Fiction. 3. Plantation life — Fiction. 4. Large type books. I. Title.
PS3566.E238F65 2004
813′.54—dc22 2004042170

Folly's Bride

National Association for Visually Handicapped
serving the partially seeing

As the Founder/CEO of NAVH, the only national health agency solely devoted to those who, although not totally blind, have an eye disease which could lead to serious visual impairment, I am pleased to recognize Thorndike Press* as one of the leading publishers in the large print field.

Founded in 1954 in San Francisco to prepare large print textbooks for partially seeing children, NAVH became the pioneer and standard setting agency in the preparation of large type.

Today, those publishers who meet our standards carry the prestigious "Seal of Approval" indicating high quality large print. We are delighted that Thorndike Press is one of the publishers whose titles meet these standards. We are also pleased to recognize the significant contribution Thorndike Press is making in this important and growing field.

Lorraine H. Marchi, L.H.D.
Founder/CEO
NAVH

* Thorndike Press encompasses the following imprints: Thorndike, Wheeler, Walker and Large Pr int Press.

A Note from the Author

Folly's Bride, the fourth book in my *Brides of Montclair* series is set in Savannah, Georgia, in 1830 — a place and time very different from our own. If the circumstances, actions, and emotions of the characters portrayed here seem somewhat extreme, it is well to keep in mind the context in which these events took place.

It has been my sincere effort in writing this series of books to maintain the integrity of the era and the historical authenticity — in other words, the backdrop against which my fictional characters move, act, and react.

Although *Folly's Bride* is a work of fiction, as are all the books in this series, many of the situations and events depicted here are based on facts. Some of my resources have been eye-witness accounts, journals, diaries, and letters written in the periods of history portrayed in the novels. The attitudes of some of the characters, the prejudices or reactions described in this book were formed by the climate of the time, the environment in which they were reared, and their early influences and experiences.

It is my hope, therefore, that you will read and enjoy Sara's story and understand better the role she plays in the later books of this series.

Jane Peart

Part I

Savannah

Summer 1830

chapter 1

"Sara! You must come out! You're wanted downstairs right away," Lucie hissed through the keyhole of the locked bedroom door. "Stepmama is furious and Father has sent word that he's coming home early from the Exchange. *She* says he's in a rage over what you've done!"

"I haven't done anything! It's not my fault if those two hotheads decide to fight a duel!" came her sister's indignant voice from the other side of the door.

"Oh, Sara, *please!*" Lucie pleaded. "Father will be here any minute. You must do as you're told!"

"I will not come down just because *she* is in a frenzy."

Lucie shifted her crouched position on the hall floor and tried again. "Well, at least let me come in," she whispered desperately.

There was a moment's silence from the room beyond, then the sound of the lock sliding back. The door inched open. With a glance over her shoulder, Lucie slipped inside. Immediately the door was shut behind her and locked again. At Lucie's entrance, Ruffy, Sara's spaniel, who was sharing his mistress's refuge, lifted his head and fixed a mournful gaze on her.

Lucie shook her head sighing, "Sara, you're so stubborn."

"No," denied Sara. "I am *strong.*"

Sara moved restlessly over to the window seat, picked up the mustard-striped cat sleeping on the cushioned sill and, nestling her in her arms, said defiantly, "No matter what *she* says, I am not going to take the blame for something I had nothing to do with —"

"*She* says you are the cause!" Lucie climbed up on Sara's high canopy bed and leaned over the footrail. "*She* says you flirted with both of them, tried to make them jealous, and laughed when Landon called Harrison out!"

"I did no such thing!"

"*She* says —"

"I don't give a fig for what *she* says. *She* wasn't there, was she? *She* always suspects the worst about me," Sara said, tossing her head, her dark curls tumbling about her shoulders. "Anyway, Father will believe me."

Sara wished she could be as sure of that fact as she tried to sound. She used to be able to count on her father's constant, if sometimes reluctant, leniency. That is, until two years ago, when he had married Georgina Nugent and brought her home to Savannah from Charleston. Now, he was more inclined to avoid conflict by accepting his new wife's version of any dispute.

Lucie was silent. There was no use arguing with Sara, no use trying to reason with her. She would always think and do exactly as she pleased. "Headstrong," their father called her. "Obstinate," Stepmama said. "Mule-headed," Mammy June, the girls' old nurse, put it less delicately.

Lucie gazed at her sister, half-admiringly, half-enviously. Even though she adored her only sister, she could not help envying her a little. She often wished her own nutmeg-brown hair were the same color as Sara's lustrous curls, that her eyelashes were as long and thick, that she had those same enchanting dimples.

There was nothing more to be said, Lucie decided. Sara would just have to get out of this predicament on her own. Not for a minute did Lucie doubt that she would.

In the meantime Sara sat staring out the window, her rebellious thoughts in sharp contrast to the serenity of the scene below. The soft breeze of the early summer afternoon stirred the purple clusters on the wisteria vine clinging to the wrought-iron balcony. And beyond, she could see the peaceful symmetry of the rows of fine houses that lined the square on which the Leightons' own handsome house faced.

Sara pursed her rosy lips in a pout. How stupid to be closeted up on a day like this when she could have been out riding or visiting or enjoying any number of pleasant pastimes. It was only to escape the incessant scolding of that impossible Georgina that Sara had barricaded herself in her room.

Just then there was the sound of carriage wheels on the street below, followed by the deep voice of their father speaking to Trent, the butler, at the front door.

The two sisters exchanged glances — Lucie's eyes, wide with apprehension; Sara's, with determination. At almost the same time footsteps tapped along the hall, accompanied by the swish of taffeta skirts, stopping outside Sara's room. Next came a rapping at the door.

"Sara Leighton, come out at once! Your father is home and waiting downstairs to speak with you." Georgina's strident tone was unmistakable.

The sisters exchanged another glance. Lucie looked anxious and Sara, resigned. She could not disobey her father's summons.

Sara rose, spilling the cat out of her lap. Moving with deliberate slowness, she went over to her dressing table and picked up her silver-backed brush. She caught a handful of dark hair and gave it a few leisurely strokes.

The impatient knock came again.

"Sara, did you hear me?"

"Yes. I'm coming."

Lucie slipped off the bed and hurried to Sara, taking both her hands. Sara's hands felt cold and suddenly clammy. She did not look forward to this encounter with her father, but she was determined not to betray her dread in front of her stepmother. Besides, she had to show Lucie not to let Georgina intimidate *her.*

"It will be all right, Lucie, don't worry," Sara assured her and swept out the door, head held high.

At the top of the curved stairway, she paused momentarily. From this vantage point she could see the imposing figure of her father standing at the white marble fireplace in the parlor. By his stance she could tell that he was very angry. When she reached the bottom step, she halted and took a deep breath before entering the room.

Georgina was seated in one of the wing chairs, flushed and frustrated, her eyes accusing as Sara came in. Ignoring her, Sara addressed her father directly.

"You wanted to see me, Papa?"

Slowly Leonard Leighton swiveled around. He controlled an involuntary gasp at the sight of his eldest daughter. Sara's extraordinary beauty never failed to shock him with her resemblance to his beloved first wife, Emma — the startling contrast of creamy, magnolia-like skin against raven black hair, the blue-violet eyes under the dark wings of her brows, the fine cameo features.

Beautiful, yes, but she was also mischievous and capricious, turning the brains of the young men who flocked around her into soft pudding, he reminded himself. Georgina had often pointed out Sara's ability to manipulate, and urged him to be firmer with her. Still, his daughter stood before him now with such a look of utter guilelessness that his heart turned over. It took all his stiffened resolve to deal with her forcefully. So he cleared his throat and attempted a proper sternness.

"What is this I am told about your inciting two young men to unlawful behavior, young lady?"

"I don't know what you mean, Papa," Sara replied meekly.

Georgina clicked her tongue. "Don't play the innocent, Sara. You know you behaved disgracefully."

Leonard turned to his wife, lifting an eyebrow. "I will handle this, my dear."

Sara threw a triumphant glance at her stepmother, and Georgina reddened.

Frowning, Leonard faced her again. "Don't you know dueling is against the law, Sara?"

"There was no duel, Papa."

"No thanks to you, I am told. The two young fools were prevented from their stupidity, but it could have ended in tragedy —"

"To say nothing of disgracing your family and ruining yourself and your sister's chances for ever being accepted in society again or achieving suitable marriages!" interjected Georgina, unable to keep quiet.

Leonard rolled his eyes. *Women!* he thought peevishly. Was there never any peace in a house with women? Especially strong-willed women like his second wife and his eldest daughter.

"Please, Georgina, my dear." He checked

his irritation with her. But he did not miss Sara's barely suppressed smile of satisfaction, and it infuriated him. Drat the girl! Why couldn't Sara be more like her sister Lucie, docile and obedient? Why did she always have to stir things up so?

"Well now, miss, no matter who is at fault in this matter, it has become the subject of public gossip. And I will not have my family touched by even a breath of scandal, do you understand?" His annoyance mounted, fueling the harsh words. "Maybe *they* have learned their lesson, but you, miss, must learn yours. There'll be no more parties, no more balls, no more chances for you to flaunt your charms upon susceptible young men for quite a while. You are confined to this house for an indeterminate period and you are to make yourself useful and helpful to your stepmother as a dutiful, submissive daughter should do."

Anger flamed in Sara, sparking all the hidden hurt and resentment she felt for the woman who had usurped her special place with her adored father, poisoning his mind against her.

"But, Papa!" she protested. "For how long?"

"For as long as I deem necessary. Sufficient time to teach you a lesson in humility and proper ladylike deportment."

Sara flashed a look of fury at her stepmother who was, she suspected, responsible for this punishment. But Georgina wore a mask of cool complacence. To Sara, she resembled a cat who had just lapped up a bowl of cream. Apparently this was the price she would exact for her stepdaughter's foolish flirtation with the two smitten beaux.

Sara clenched her hands at her sides. It was so unfair. "But, Papa, I'm to be in Katherine Maitland's wedding next month!"

"Well, we shall see —" Leonard commented noncommittally.

"I'm one of the bridesmaids, Papa," she pressed, "and the dresses are already being made —"

"I *said* — we shall see, Sara." Her father scowled, looking toward his wife for some direction. But Georgina, pretending great concentration on her needlepoint, did not reply.

"Papa —" Sara hesitated. She would *not* beg. Not in front of Georgina.

"That is all for now, Sara." Leonard turned his back so as not to see the plea in those eyes.

Mutinous and angry, Sara stood a minute longer, torn between blind rage and self-pity. If her father were alone, she felt sure she could reach him, appeal to him to temper her sentence or, at the very least, give her a date that it would come to an end! But the implacable Georgina sat there, unmoved by Sara's obvious distress and her husband's discomfort.

Sara waited a moment longer, then whirled around and walked out of the room in a flurry of petticoats.

I'll find a way, she promised herself. *They can't keep me a prisoner indefinitely.*

She started upstairs and saw Lucie's little face pressed between the banisters of the balcony overlooking the center hall. She had probably been straining to hear what was going on, eavesdropping on the scene taking place in the parlor.

Sara felt a rush of affection for her younger sister. They had been through so much together. First, their mother's death after a long, agonizing illness. Afterwards, the neglect of their bereaved, distracted father, who had left them in the care of indulgent servants and their Negro mammy. Then came the shock of his remarriage. When Georgina arrived, they suffered her dominating presence together, together experienced the misery of being uprooted from home and sent away to boarding school. Through all the trauma of their young lives it was their closeness that made all the changes endurable.

When she reached the top of the stairs, she gave Lucie a hug.

"Oh, Sara, what did they do to you?"

"Forty lashes!" she quipped, then laughed at Lucie's stricken expression. "Don't look so sad. I'll be all right. Papa will come around."

Sara was already planning her strategy. She did not underestimate her adversary. Georgina was a formidable foe. But Sara knew her father. She would break down his façade of disapproval and win him back. It might take a little longer than usual this time because of the silly actions of Landon Buehl and Harrison Mills. Still, she could try.

So far, the duel was only a rumor. She knew for a fact that her name had not even been mentioned in the quarrel. Even though Savannah loved a "good gossip," some other escapade would soon become the topic of drawing room conversation. Thank goodness, no real harm had been done.

She would do her penance, Sara decided. She would act the part of a "dutiful daughter" as her father had directed. She was really quite good at playacting, having taken some of the lead roles in the tableaux and plays at boarding school. Not only that, but she had had plenty of practice in masking her true feelings at home these past two years. She would not give Georgina the satisfaction of reporting a single impertinence, misdeed, or disobedient action.

Of one thing Sara was certain. She was *not* going to miss being in Katherine Maitland's wedding to Douglas Cameron of Virginia. Not with Theo coming all the way from Charleston!

chapter 2

Sara locked her bedroom door and moved swiftly over to the small fruitwood desk designed with inlaid marquetry. She touched the hidden spring that opened the secret drawer and brought out the packet concealed within. Taking it over to the window seat, she curled up, untied the ribbon that bound it, and read over Theo's letters, one by one.

"My darling Sara, you have only been away from Charleston for two weeks, but it has seemed a lifetime —" *How beautifully Theo expressed himself,* Sara thought, *how poetic and romantic!*

She closed her eyes briefly, holding the letter to her breast, and letting her mind rush back to the very first time she had ever laid eyes on Theo Richardson.

It was Visitors' Day at Madame Couvoisier's Academe, at least for the boarding students lucky enough to have relatives or friends in the Charleston area. The unfortunate few who were not expecting guests often crowded onto the balcony overlooking the front lawn and gardens to watch the arrivals. Seeking diversion from an otherwise boring Sunday afternoon, Sara had joined them.

It was Georgina, of course, who had insisted that young ladies of Sara's and Lucie's ages needed proper "finishing." It was at her direction that they had been dispatched to the Academe soon after her marriage to their father. Sara was still unreconciled to her forced exile from Savannah. That is, until that Sunday afternoon, when Theo's entrance into her life changed things. Forever.

She thought of it now. He had come bounding up the wide veranda steps at the very instant Sara leaned over the balustrade. Afterwards she declared to Lucie it must have been fate that assigned her to that spot, for he had glanced up, caught her eye, and smiled. He was undeniably the most striking man who had ever set foot on the campus, she was sure. So deeply bronzed was his skin, so black his wavy hair that the bright blue of his eyes was a shock to the senses and the whiteness of even teeth, a surprise. But it was the roguish expression in those eyes that took Sara's breath away.

As their gaze met and held, there was about that moment a sense of recognition and inevitability.

He took off his wide-brimmed, straw hat, and bowed slightly, almost mockingly. Mesmerized, Sara could only stare.

She had no excuse to go downstairs into the parlor where guests were received, so all she could do was wonder who he was and whom he had come to visit.

To her astonishment, Katherine Maitland, an older student, sought her out after visiting hours.

"Theo Richardson wants to meet you, Sara," she said. "He and my cousin Shelton went to school together in Virginia, so Theo is on the approved guest list. If you like, I can place your name with mine to receive him next Visitors' Day."

Barely disguising her excitement at the invitation, Sara had agreed. First, she was wild to meet the young man formally, and second, to be singled out by one of the most popular girls at the Academe gave Sara a status she might not otherwise have attained.

Sara opened her eyes and reread the letter she held. Its bold handwriting brought Theo's image vividly to mind.

She recalled that the very next Sunday

Theo, looking outrageously handsome in a light blue coat, frilled shirt, and plum-colored silk cravat, was in the first flow of arrivals. He was carrying two small bouquets; one he gave to Katherine and the other he handed to Sara, bending over her hand and kissing her fingertips. Katherine had then discreetly disappeared, leaving them alone to get acquainted in the garden, shielded by the flowering azalea bushes from the eagle-eyed chaperone presiding over the girls and their callers. They had strolled along flower-lined paths together.

Their rapport was instant, their compatibility immediate — both, rebels; both, iconoclasts; both, reckless and impatient with rules and regulations.

What Sara remembered most about that afternoon was a sense of heightened awareness. Everything was more intense — the fragrance of the flowers, the leafy canopy of the overarching trees, the glistening water where Madame Couvoisier's imported swans glided, and Theo beside her. On that sun-gilded afternoon, Sara fell in love.

After that, Theo came every Visitors' Day on the pretext of visiting his friend's cousin. In reality, it was Sara with whom he spent the two allotted hours.

Quickly they got to know each other, their

words tumbling over one another in their eagerness to learn everything about their companion. Sara confided her unhappiness, her feelings of abandonment after her father's remarriage, her homesickness and loneliness for Savannah.

In return, Theo told her he had been born and brought up in Jamaica on a sugar plantation belonging to his grandfather. He hinted that things had not gone well there and that the family had returned to Charleston, where his mother had inherited a house on the island across from the Ashley River. As a boy, he had loved exploring its banks, fishing, swimming, crabbing, and then he had been sent away to school in Virginia when he was eleven.

"I hated school! I loathed everything about it," he confessed. "The regimen, the discipline, my studies, the way the older boys bullied the younger ones. In fact, I got into so many fights defending the weaker fellows that the headmaster threatened to expel me. I was allowed to come home, but when I got there —" He paused, his eyes clouding over — "my father had left, though Mother never explained why."

Sara felt a surge of pity for the young Theo facing such tragedy. She put out a hand and touched his sleeve lightly.

He had jumped up then, deliberately masking the pain with a studied attempt at levity. "Isn't there something about letting the 'dead past bury its dead'? If I had applied myself to my studies at the University of South Carolina, I might have been able to recall the quote. Or, for that matter, to pursue the real interest of my life — architecture. Of course, I never mastered the necessary mathematics." He gave an apologetic laugh. Taking his seat again, his gaze caressed Sara's features. "You see, I worship beauty in all forms. Anything that is coarse or ugly or out of proportion is an anathema to me. On the other hand, perfection inspires the artist in me."

Enthralled, Sara had listened. Often while he talked, Theo sketched, with Sara as his subject. Once he had sketched her in the garden by the lily pond and, although he had not been satisfied with his effort, she begged him to give the drawing to her.

Sara had framed it, but kept it concealed under the pillow of the window seat. She took it out now and looked at it, remembering Theo's graceful hand moving across the paper, holding the stick of charcoal. How often she had longed to smooth back the wayward lock of hair that fell forward over his brow as he bent over his drawing pad, but she had refrained.

When school ended in the spring, Sara returned home for the summer. Since it wouldn't do for Georgina to know about the courtship, Sara had arranged for their secret correspondence, with the complicity of a day student who enclosed Theo's letters in hers to Sara. In turn, Sara enclosed her letters to Theo in the ones she wrote to her friend. Otherwise, she knew, her stepmother would have felt it her parental duty to open the letters and read them before passing them on to Sara.

At the end of the summer, Katherine Maitland, who had finished at the Academe, made her debut to which Sara was invited. A number of parties in Katherine's honor were given as well, and Sara was included in all of them, a fact due more to Kate's friendship with Theo, than to Sara.

Sara rifled through Theo's letters to find the one written before that event.

> I am counting the hours until I see you again in Savannah," he wrote. "It seems a thousand years since I saw your face, held your hands, kissed your lips. How could one small person so fill a man's heart and mind?

His words brought back all the excitement of that enchanted week. She and Theo were together constantly — dancing, managing to slip away in the midst of the ball to rendezvous in the garden or on the veranda, sitting together at the melodrama performed aboard the showboat *Golden Slipper* moored in Savannah harbor, eating together at barbeques and dinner parties. And at every opportunity, exchanging kisses full of sweetness and promise.

Unconsciously, Sara placed her fingers lightly on her lips, tracing their outline. She recalled each of Theo's kisses, from the first hasty one, stolen in the arbor of the Academe garden, until the farewell kiss before her departure for Savannah a few weeks earlier.

That kiss summed up the past year of Sunday visits and long walks, of secret meetings, and smuggled love letters. Sara now knew that what they felt for each other transcended mutual attraction and infatuation, and the idea sent her head spinning dizzily.

"Sara! Sara, may I come in?" Lucie's soft voice drew Sara back to the present. Hastily she bundled up the packet of letters, shoved them back into the secret drawer, and pressed the spring that secured it.

"Just a minute, Lucie."

She went over and slid back the latch, opening the door for her younger sister.

"Why do you have the door locked, Sara?" Lucie seemed puzzled.

"Can't I have a little privacy once in a while?" She deftly dodged the issue. "What do you want?"

"Stepmama sent me to tell you we're having company for dinner and she wants you to come down early and help entertain."

Sara groaned. Still, she knew she must be very careful not to do or say anything that would upset Georgina and bring further punishment or an extension of the one already pronounced.

All these weeks Sara had stayed out of her stepmother's way as much as possible. Besides attending church on Sundays with Georgina and Lucie, the only outing she was allowed was an early morning horseback ride, after which she reported to Georgina's boudoir to receive instructions for the day. She had learned to accept whatever chores she was assigned, no matter how tiresome, without a murmur of complaint.

So far, much to everyone's amazement, Sara had been the epitome of affability and irreproachable conduct. She mustn't spoil that spotless record. Sighing heavily, she said to Lucie, "Tell her I'll be downstairs at six."

As promised, Sara appeared promptly in the parlor just as the ormolu clock on the mantle was striking the hour, and graciously greeted the guests. At the dinner table she was quiet, demure, never offering an opinion nor speaking her mind in her usual, spritely manner. She could see that it irritated Georgina to have to carry the entire burden of conversation. And throughout the meal, her father cast curious, then annoyed, glances in her direction, puzzled by her uncharacteristic silence.

Sara was playing the submissive daughter to the hilt. She knew, sooner or later, that her father's patience would be frayed and he would lift her "house arrest."

But, in spite of all her effort, or maybe because Leonard Leighton suspected the games she was playing, to Sara's chagrin she was not relieved of her imprisonment until the week before Katherine's wedding. This she laid directly to the hand of her stepmother. Georgina was vindictive; Sara had always known that. The fact that she was determined to exact "the last pound of flesh" from her willful stepdaughter did not surprise Sara at all.

Sara Leighton always relied on her first impressions, no matter how many times she had been cautioned that first impressions were often misleading. Nevertheless, they had proved true as far as Georgina was concerned. The moment she had laid eyes on her stepmother, Sara had felt a cold dislike. And as time went on, she had found the hostility was mutual.

Released at last from her month-long confinement, Sara's joy knew no bounds. Soon would begin the round of prenuptial parties to which all the bridesmaids and the men in the wedding party would be invited. It would be a week of frolic, festivity, and fun. Most of all she was counting the days until her reunion with Theo.

When would he arrive? Sara wondered. She had not heard from him in weeks. Why had he not written? Maybe because he knew he would soon be in Savannah, that they would be together again. Maybe because he wanted to avoid risking detection of their romance before he had a chance to present himself to her parents. Whatever the reason, Sara was eager to see him.

Though she would miss his romantic letters and their surreptitious meetings of the past year, she was anxious to arrange for her father to meet Theo. Then he could request permission to call and thus legitimize their secret love. She was sure that, once Theo worked his charm on her parents, any reservation about his calling on her would vanish. Georgina, who in Sara's opinion, was an "unmitigated snob," would surely be impressed with Theo's Maitland connection.

On the other hand, she allowed herself a moment of doubt. How would her father feel about a man with no profession, no formal education, no "prospects" to speak of? His interest in the arts Leonard Leighton might consider "unmanly." Still, Sara, with her ability to see things the way she wanted them to be, did not dwell long on the unlikely possibility that Theo would not be welcome in their home.

Lucie was the only one who knew her secret. Perhaps Katherine Maitland had guessed. Sara even wondered if being asked to be one of Katherine's twelve bridesmaids might not have been made at Theo's request, since she and Katherine were not especially close. He had been a classmate of both her cousin Shelton and Douglas Cameron at the school in Virginia, and was to be one of Doug's groomsmen.

On the morning of the first ball given in honor of the engaged couple, Sara was awake early. By now, members of the wedding party had already begun to arrive. Had Theo come? How could she wait until evening to see him?

Too restless to stay in bed any longer, Sara got up and sent word to the stables to have her horse, Princess, saddled and brought around by seven. She buttoned a lightweight blue jacket over a muslin blouse, slipped on a short riding skirt, then tied back her hair with a geranium-red ribbon. This early, no one would be about to see her without a proper riding habit, she thought.

Boots in hand so as not to disturb the still sleeping household, Sara slipped down the stairway. A coffee urn stood on the buffet in the dining room, and Sara poured herself a cup, added cream, then walked over to the window.

While she sipped the hot coffee, she looked out on one of the prettiest residential squares of Savannah. Across the street she could see the neighbors' houseboy, Caleb, sweeping the front steps of the fine Regency mansion, almost a twin to the Leightons' own house, both designed twenty years before by a famous English architect.

Then seeing her groom leading a sleek ginger mare to the mounting block in front of the house, Sara put down her cup and hurried outside.

The morning air was cool, scented with the sweetness of azaleas and the heavy fragrance of magnolias. Sara trotted along the quiet, brick-paved streets, shaded by live oaks draped with Spanish moss, past the stately homes, almost all of them occupied by families she had known all her life. It felt good to be back in her hometown. She had missed it so all the months she had been away in Charleston.

At the end of the road, she turned her horse away from town toward the less crowded countryside, heading out toward the bluff above the river.

Sara never felt freer, happier than when on horseback. There was a wild streak in her that railed against the conventions, dress, and protocol of her social status and sex. Sometimes, she longed to have the complete freedom that she saw in her young stepbrothers when they were out from under the eye of their watchful mother. Scott and Bowen Nugent, nine and eleven, Georgina's sons by her first marriage, lived most of the time with their paternal grandmother on an island plantation across the inlet from Charleston. They visited their mother in Savannah on school holidays and for a few weeks in summer. But all males, despite having to observe the proprieties in the parlor, were allowed a freedom elsewhere that Sara often envied.

Now, giving Princess her head, Sara felt the wind in her face, whipping her hair back and dislodging the scrap of bright ribbon that bound it. Almost giddy with happiness, she bent low over her horse, feeling the strong rhythm of muscle and sinew. When at length she pulled her mare to a halt high up on the hill overlooking the bay where ships, small and large, nestled close to the wharves lining the shore, Sara was breathless from the exhilaration of the run.

Suddenly a deep male voice broke her reverie. "Good morning."

Startled, Sara turned in her saddle and saw a young man dismounting from a white horse a few feet behind her.

A ridiculous urge to giggle welled up inside. All she could think of was Lucie's daydream. Lucie, addicted to romantic novels, would be sure to make something of this unexpected encounter. Surely this self-assured rider was the handsome knight on the white charger, sent to rescue Sara from their wicked stepmother! Of course, Lucie would come along when he carried Sara off to live in a beautiful castle far away. She fought to suppress a smile.

The sunlight was dazzling, shining on the water below, and creating an aura of gold about the young man's russet-brown hair as he bared his head and made Sara a sweeping bow.

"May I take the liberty of introducing myself," he asked, quickly adding, "we have mutual acquaintances. The Maitlands. I'm here for Miss Katherine's wedding to my friend, Douglas Cameron. I'm Clayborn Montrose."

Sara inclined her head slightly as she gave him a silent appraisal. He stood over six feet tall, nicely proportioned, his features strong yet refined. His warm brown eyes held both intelligence and humor.

"You gave me quite a chase," he remarked. "I was leaving my host's house at the time you came out your gate. You are a remarkable rider, Miss Leighton."

"I wasn't aware we were acquainted, Mr. Montrose. Who, pray tell, is your host?"

"The Pierce family is related to Douglas. We are staying with them during the wedding week." He paused and again Sara noticed the laughter in his eyes even as he flushed a little under his healthy tan. "We saw you in your carriage Sunday morning, accompanied by two other ladies — perhaps your sister, your mother?"

"My *stepmother,*" corrected Sara sharply.

"I asked Fax Pierce the identity of the three lovely ladies and he told us. He also told me you rode every morning . . . *early.*" He paused. "Do forgive my boldness, but knowing we would meet later in the day anyway, since we are both members of the wedding party, I was forward enough to bypass a formal introduction. I hope you won't hold it against me."

Sara said nothing. She would let him squirm for his brashness, she decided. She would be nothing if not proper and ladylike. If this meeting ever got back to Georgina, there would be the devil to pay. She wasn't going to risk being kept home from the ball tonight by this careless stranger's overstepping of the bounds of propriety.

Sara picked up her reins, gave Princess a little slap on her flank with her riding crop, and turned her past Clayborn and his white steed, cantering off without a backward glance. So much for knights on white chargers, she thought with a laugh. Wait until I tell Lucie!

She was unaware of Clayborn Montrose staring after her, his expression a mixture of disappointment and unabashed admiration.

chapter 3

"Oh, Sara, you look beautiful!" Lucie exclaimed from her vantage point at the end of Sara's bed as she watched her sister dress for the ball.

Sara twirled before the mirror. "Do I?"

It was not mere vanity that prompted Sara's question. Even though she had heard those words over and over since she was a little girl, Sara needed especially to believe them tonight. When she saw Theo for the first time in over two months, she must *feel* beautiful.

She stopped pirouetting and studied her reflection critically. Her cheeks were flushed with excitement, her eyes sparkling with anticipation. She touched the shiny curls tied with blue satin ribbons and bunched over her ears, then held out the flounced skirt and tried a few dance steps.

Her gown was a fantasy of blue tulle and lace embroidery, one of several that had been made for Sara. It was a matter of pride to Georgina that her stepdaughter be appropriately gowned for every occasion during this week of festive events before Katherine Maitland's wedding. Therefore, she had spared no expense in either materials or dressmaking costs.

"Come here, Lucie, help me fasten this." Sara picked up a delicate gold filigree necklace from the top of her dressing table.

Eagerly Lucie complied with her sister's request. She loved being part of Sara's life. She hoped it was a kind of preview of her own life in another few years. But, the difference in their ages was not all. She would probably never be a belle like Sara, with dozens of beaux. Lucie gave a little sigh as she did the clasp, then watched as Sara slipped in matching earrings.

"Now, I'm ready, I think." Sara stepped back and viewed her reflection once more.

"Your gloves!" cried Lucie, handing her long white kid ones.

"Thank you!" Sara smiled fondly at her younger sister who was gazing at her in such dazzled delight.

"And your fan! Sara, don't forget your fan!" reminded Lucie as Sara started for the door.

"You're a dear, Lucie. Whatever would I

do without you?" Sara laughed, patting the rosy cheek.

"I'm going to wait up to hear all about everything!"

"But it will be quite late, Lucie!"

"I'll make myself stay awake. I won't dare fall asleep," she promised.

Sara blew her a kiss and floated out of the room. Her father, in evening dress, stood in the hall, holding his watch and glaring upward. But when he saw the vision descending the stairs, his annoyed frown vanished.

He complimented her extravagantly and offered his arm to escort her to the waiting carriage. Even Georgina, looking on as they left, felt a smug satisfaction that no other young lady at the ball would hold a candle to her stepdaughter.

Sara sat on the edge of the carriage seat all the way to the Maitlands' town house. Lights winked out from every window, and Sara's heart was fluttering like a wild bird as they approached the Oglethorpe Square mansion. Soon, soon, she would see Theo!

They could hear the music as the carriage stopped in front, and Sara felt an anticipatory tingle. Soon she would be dancing with Theo!

On her father's arm Sara mounted the

"welcoming arms" steps and entered the foyer, brilliant with lighted chandeliers. Mr. and Mrs. Maitland, Katherine, and a tall, sandy-haired young man stood in the entrance hall to receive their guests. Sara murmured something polite to Katherine's parents and greeted Katherine, all the time distractedly wondering where Theo was.

"Sara, this is my fiancé, Douglas Cameron," Katherine was saying. Then, turning to the young man at her side, she said, "Doug, may I present Miss Sara Leighton?"

Sara felt her hand suddenly encased in a strong clasp.

Looking down at her from his great height, Douglas Cameron acknowledged the introduction with a teasing twinkle in his eyes. "I feel as if I know you, Miss Sara. Since early morning I have heard nothing else but enthusiastic accounts of your beauty and your grace on horseback."

Sara gazed up at him blankly. "But, how —"

"My good friend, Clay Montrose, has been completely smitten and is impatiently awaiting your arrival. If you don't want your entire dance card scribbled with his name, I warn you to hide it." Douglas grinned.

There was no time for further talk because other guests were behind her in the receiving line. Her father touched her arm, saying, "Hurry along, Sara." Douglas released her hand, and she moved away.

Where was Theo? Sara wondered, while with a practiced smile on her face, she acknowledged greetings. She moved confidently from one small group to the other, collecting a handful of admiring young men along the way. Even as Sara kept up the repartee expected on such social occasions, her gaze swept the room, looking for him.

From the other side of the room Clayborn Montrose saw Sara enter the room. He felt his heart leap, and his fingers tightened around the glass he was holding. She was even lovelier than he remembered. He watched as she glanced around the room, her exquisite head turning this way and that. Then she seemed to look in his direction. As her face lighted up, a thrill of hope spread all through Clay. He started forward. Then, realizing that her gaze was going beyond him over his shoulder, he halted and turned in time to see a slim, dark-haired young man pass him and hurry toward Sara.

As Sara saw Theo coming toward her, her joy was so intense she could not think of a thing to say. But what his eyes told her needed no words.

"May I have this dance, Miss Sara?" he asked, and she did not remember taking his hand or moving with him onto the dance floor. All she was conscious of was the ecstasy of being in his arms.

In another moment the two of them were on the dance floor. Sara was moving with easy grace, her belled skirt swaying in a shimmering blue sheen, her expression blissful, her smile radiant.

All evening Clay watched her go from partner to partner, most often with the handsome, dark fellow with whom she seemed most vivacious. With all his heart, Clay hoped fervently that he had not met Sara Leighton too late, that she was not promised to someone else. The possibility that he might lose her before he had even had a chance to win her tormented him. From the first moment he had laid eyes upon her he knew that she was the woman he had dreamed all his life of finding.

The ball was over, and her father had come to take her home. Sara, with one reluctant, lingering look at Theo, had gone with Mr. Leighton to bid their hosts good-night. Theo had written something on the back of her dance card, but she had not had a chance to read it. When he gave it to her, she slipped it inside her glove.

"Tired?" her father asked, noticing her unusual silence once they were in the carriage. "I noticed you didn't miss a dance," he chuckled.

Sara nodded dreamily. She was far from tired. Over-stimulated would more aptly describe the way she felt. It had been an evening beyond her dreams. She and Theo had even managed to slip away into the Maitlands' garden for a few minutes alone.

On the pretext of going to the ladies' "refreshing" room, Sara had turned instead and gone through the open French doors out to the spot where Theo waited, hidden. He had whispered her name, and she was at once swept into his embrace.

They had not dared risk more than a few minutes' absence. If Sara were missed, she knew tongues would wag. Spiteful gossip and malicious speculation could ruin her reputation. People, especially jealous girls who did not like her, were always quick to jump to conclusions. They loved to pass along a juicy tidbit that would take her out of circulation and improve their own romantic prospects.

But before they returned to the ballroom separately, Theo said, "Sara, we must arrange to meet. Alone. Where we can talk."

"I'll ask my father if you may call," Sara replied breathlessly.

"No!" His reply was so adamant it startled her. "It must be somewhere away from prying eyes, curious ears." There was an unusual urgency in his voice. "I have something I need to tell you —"

"I'll see. I'll try," Sara said hurriedly. She glanced nervously back toward the lighted windows of the ballroom. If someone saw them out here together —

"Sara, it's important," Theo insisted.

"Yes, I understand." Her heart was pounding, her head swam. Surely Theo meant to declare himself. Oh, heavens! it was all coming true! she thought deliriously. "Yes, yes. I'll find a way. Send word. But we must go in now!"

Sara could not wait to reach home, and in the privacy of her bedroom, to read what Theo had written.

When she went upstairs a candle was still burning on her dressing table, the wax running into puddles, the flame sputtering. She had forgotten Lucie's promise to wait up. But she saw that her younger sister had not been able to stay awake and was curled up on top of Sara's bed, the quilt pulled over her.

Sara drifted into the room, tossing her

cape onto a chair where it slipped to the floor. Flushed and dreamy-eyed, she spun to the center of the room and began untying the ribbons that held her ringlets, then shook out her hair until it fell cascading about her shoulders. Slowly she began unfastening her long French gloves, peeling them off and carelessly flinging them to follow her cape. Then she stood quite still and closed her eyes, clutching her dance card to her breast. Theo!

Moving over to the dimming light of the candle, she read the words he had scribbled on the card.

In the guest room of the Pierce residence a few streets away, Clayborn Montrose lay awake, staring into the darkness and thinking about Sara Leighton.

He was obsessed with her. How else could he explain the compelling power she had had over his thoughts from almost the first moment he had seen her?

He had been lucky to have one dance with her this evening, if you could call it that. During the Paul Jones, he had maneuvered himself opposite her when the music stopped and had gone one round of the dance floor before the caller signaled the musicians to start another circle.

Before going to bed, he had written in his journal:

> To be near her is absolute enchantment. The scent of her skin is like ambrosia. Her hair, like midnight silk. With a single look she drew me into the deep, mysterious blue depths of her eyes. She is the loveliest creature I have ever seen. How I know, I can only guess, but I feel that she is destined to be my bride. Her name is Sara Leighton.

Aunt Avril, his adopted mother, had encouraged the habit of keeping a journal from the time he had first come to live with her and Uncle Graham at Montclair when he was eleven years old. He had been diligent in the practice all the time he was away at school and later when he attended William and Mary College in Williamsburg. In it, he had learned to confide his inmost thoughts, his intimate feelings, his deepest beliefs.

Now, it was second nature to carry the leather-bound book with him whenever he traveled. Each Christmas Aunt Avril gave him a new one for the year to come.

"I have kept a journal most of my life," she had told him. "And I have never been sorry. It's a way to discover yourself and chart your spiritual progress."

Clay agreed with her. But now what was he to do with this hope that burned within him? A hope in which there seemed no possibility of its becoming reality?

Young and inexperienced as he was, Clay knew this rushing emotion he felt was unusual. He was under some kind of spell from which he did not want to extricate himself.

Once, when he had been talking to Aunt Avril about her marriage to Uncle Graham, she had said, "A lifelong love has to be based on mutual, shared belief. That is the first and most important thing." He knew their story, for Avril had told him all about it. She had loved Graham since she was a young girl and he had loved her, too. It was at first a strong friendship, then it had become something more — a relationship tested by time, trials, many separations, and misunderstandings. "Because our love was right and good, because it was meant to be, God allowed us to come together," Avril had concluded happily.

Clay knew that what he felt for Sara Leighton at this point was more emotion than time-tested love. They had not had an opportunity to know each other. There was only this strong, instinctive feeling that somehow they were to belong together. How and when this would all come about, he had no idea.

He smiled into the darkness, remembering what Aunt Avril would probably suggest, as she did for any problem he had had through the years: "Pray about it, Clay dear. If it is in God's plan for your life, it will come to be." Then she would quote him chapter and verse.

Finally Clay closed his eyes. His last thought before drifting into sleep was of Sara Leighton.

chapter 4

The next morning when two bouquets arrived for Miss Sara Leighton, Mammy June lumbered up the stairs to deliver them to Sara's bedroom.

Propping herself up on snowy pillows, Sara responded drowsily to the knock at the door. But when she saw Mammy June, she brushed her hair out of her eyes and reached eagerly for the dainty nosegays tied with lace streamers. Breathing in the scent, Sara looked at her old nurse.

"No cards?" she asked.

Mammy June pursed her lips, folded her arms, and gave an emphatic nod of her turbaned head before replying. "Yes'm. Dey wuz cards. But Miss Georgina done took 'em to see who de flowers wuz from."

Sara felt the familiar sense of outrage. Tossing aside the covers, she started to get up when her stepmother appeared in the doorway.

Georgina held up one of the two small

cards in her hand. "Who is Theo Richardson, Sara, and why is he sending you flowers?"

An indignant retort sprang to mind, but Sara bit her lip before blurting it out, instead forcing herself to reply evenly, "He's one of the groomsmen in Katherine's wedding, a school friend of her fiancé, Douglas Cameron. We met when I was at the Academy. Last night at the ball we renewed our acquaintance."

Georgina lifted her eyebrows, but made no comment. She just held up another card. "And Clayborn Montrose?"

Sara's eyes widened in surprise. *What a persistent fellow!* she thought to herself. But she answered promptly. "He's a houseguest of the Pierces. And Douglas Cameron's best man."

"They have both asked to call," Georgina told her. "Of course, I shall have to ask your father if he wishes us to receive them."

That settled, Georgina scanned the room, taking in the discarded clothing from the night before, the general disarray. "It is time you were up, bathed and dressed, Sara," she said sharply. "Miss Holgrath will be here at eleven for your piano lesson. And Mammy June, get this awful clutter tidied up right away!"

With that, she left the room. Though Sara knew better than to voice her opinion of her stepmother to a servant, the black woman's expression left no doubt as to how *she* felt about her mistress.

Furthermore, Sara knew it would not be her father who made the final decision. He would simply defer to his wife in this matter as he had so many times before. He relinquished all matters of the social amenities regarding his daughters to Georgina.

Now that Sara knew who had sent them, she could guess the secret message of both bouquets. All young people of the time were familiar with the romantic language of flowers.

Surely the one from Theo, of scarlet roses, white alyssum, and maidenhair fern meant love and desire, worth beyond beauty, and cautious discretion.

The other one of yellow daffodils, blue forget-me-nots, and white snowdrops from the gentlemanly, but assured, Clayborn Montrose spoke honestly of his attraction, his regard, his intentions, his true love, and hope.

"Doan look lak nobody kin do nuthin' round chere no more 'thout Miss Georgina's say-so," Mammy June muttered to herself as she poured hot water into the copper tub for Sara's bath.

Sara twisted her waist-length hair into a topknot to avoid getting it wet and, preoccupied with her own thoughts, paid little attention to the old woman's mumblings. She knew Mammy June, who had been charged with the care of both sisters during the years Mr. Leighton was a widower, resented Georgina's high-handed ways as much as Sara did. Besides, what might not be tolerated in another servant was forgiven Mammy June.

But from experience Sara knew when and when not to take a stand against her stepmother. This was not the time to challenge Georgina. Sweetness and light, that was the path to take. Nothing must prevent Theo's being received. Therefore, it was extremely important that everything be done in compliance with all Georgina's rules of etiquette, since disregarding them would be sure to incur her father's displeasure. No, Sara would simply swallow her pride again. It would be worth it when Theo was received and accepted as a suitor for her hand in marriage.

Driving up from the Exchange, Leonard Leighton looked forward to a leisurely midday meal at home — reading the daily paper beforehand, enjoying a brandy and a good Havana cigar afterwards, then perhaps having a brief nap before returning to his office.

It had been a fine morning, he thought with satisfaction. The price of cotton was high and things were going very well. At forty-two, Leonard had made a place for himself in the world of Savannah commerce. Sure of his position in society, he had also prospered in business without losing the prestige of his old family name.

Of course, he had had his share of problems — losing his wife at an early age and being left a widower with the responsibility of two small daughters. With Georgina, however, that part of his life was more than satisfactory.

All in all, Leonard was feeling pleased with himself as his carriage came up on Bay Street, glad that he had moved as a young man from the Low Country of South Carolina to the small but thriving town of Savannah, Georgia.

Savannah! What a beautiful place to live. Ideally situated on forty-foot bluffs overlooking the Savannah River, with its deepwater harbor a gateway to the world of shipping and international trade. A city of commerce, true, with the warehouses along the bay and handsome public buildings like the Customs House and Courthouse, but also a city magnificently laid out in a chessboard of squares bordered by blossoming shrubs and flowers. It was those flowers that made the town a veritable garden now in the full bloom of early summer — oleander and azaleas adding color and fragrance. Live oaks, draped with lacy Spanish moss, provided shady places to rest on the benches beneath.

Beyond all that, Savannah, peopled with gracious society and filled with lovely churches such as the one the Leightons attended where George Whitfield himself had preached, was the perfect town in which to bring up a family. Other denominations, too, were represented, which spoke well of Savannah's illustrious founder, James Oglethorpe, who not only believed in religious tolerance but practiced it as well. And, of course, the charming residential areas were studded with stately houses, some of which had been designed by John Jay, the famous architect, whose distinctive touch could be seen in the decorative grilled ironwork balconies and secret walled gardens.

Indeed, his own home compared favorably with any of them, Leonard thought with a touch of pride as his carriage drew up in front of an impressive whitewashed brick mansion.

The carriage door was opened by Raleigh, the Negro coachman, smart in a bright blue coat, immaculate white linen, and black top hat, who offered a white-gloved hand to help him out. Then, as if she had been on the lookout for his noon arrival, a housemaid in starched white apron and turban opened the door just as Leonard started up the front steps.

"Afternoon, suh." She curtsied, smiling.

"Afternoon, Fronsy." Leonard handed her his hat and cane and walked into the small room off the hall adjacent to the drawing room that was his private parlor. The newspaper, crisply folded, lay on the marble-top table. He picked it up, settling himself in a tufted armchair, unfolded it, and scanned the headlines before turning to the financial pages.

From somewhere in the house he heard the sound of a piano. He smiled to himself. *One of the girls,* he thought complacently, pleased that they were both so accomplished, albeit at no small expense. He calculated mentally — music lessons, dancing classes, the school in Charleston with its outrageous fees.

Leonard winced as a discordant note was

struck, followed by a fumbling recovery. *Must be Sara,* he thought, turning the page. Sara was bored by scales, hated practicing. She had neither the patience nor the inclination to study hard enough to become proficient. It was Lucie he usually asked to play for his guests, certain that the piece would be executed well, if not brilliantly.

Sara! Leonard frowned. The girl was a puzzle. Something always brewing just below the surface.

Just then there was a light but insistent tap at his door. Leonard scowled and rustled his paper, annoyed at the interruption. Couldn't a man have a few minutes of peace in his own house?

The door pushed open and Georgina came in. "Am I disturbing you, dear?" she asked.

Dinner was always served promptly at one-fifteen in the graciously appointed dining room of the Leighton house. Its pale green painted walls and jalousied windows, their slotted panels now closed, provided a welcome oasis from the midday heat outside.

Sara and Lucie sat opposite each other at the table set with fine handpainted porcelain, embroidered linen, and gleaming silver. Georgina presided over the serving from the sideboard by Trent, the butler and houseman. At a lift of her finger, she indicated what dishes were to be brought and offered, first to Mr. Leighton at the head, then to the girls in turn.

Today's first course was a chilled orange-lemon soup, followed by a squash souffle, fresh asparagus, cold sliced ham, and hot biscuits. When the dinner plates were taken away, crystal finger bowls were brought. Finally, a deep cut-glass dish of fresh sliced peaches was placed in front of Georgina. From this, she spooned individual portions into smaller dessert bowls.

"Sara —" Georgina addressed her in the tone Sara had grown to dread, since it usually signaled some unpleasant topic. "I have spoken to your father on the matter of the two gentlemen who wish to call on you."

Sara felt the gentle pressure of Lucie's foot on her own under the table and knew she had a staunch ally in whatever was to follow.

"We —" Georgina began, then amended, "*your father* has given permission for Mr. Montrose to be received since the Faxton Pierce family are longtime friends and Mr. Montrose is their houseguest." She paused, momentarily concentrating on handing the dessert plates to Trent, who hovered nearby, ready to serve them.

Sara clenched her napkin tightly in her lap, holding her breath for Georgina's next pronouncement. It seemed her stepmother was being deliberately slow.

"But I'm afraid," Georgina continued, "that we must refuse to receive Mr. Richardson."

At this, Sara lost her usual caution and blurted out, "But why not?"

Georgina looked startled. She drew herself up, regarding Sara coldly. "We consider Mr. Richardson unsuitable."

"Unsuitable? What can you mean by *unsuitable?* Theo is a perfect gentleman with beautiful manners and a charming personality! Why would you not receive him?"

Georgina raised her eyebrows. "Are you questioning your father's decision, Sara?"

Sara flushed and darted a quick look at her father who had halted the progress of his spoon to his mouth to look at her, aghast.

"It's not that!" she protested. "It's just that neither of you has met him. It's simply not fair to pass judgment on someone you don't even know!"

"Your stepmother's opinion is all that is necessary, Sara," Mr. Leighton said gruffly.

"But she —" Sara bit her lip, then turned

to Georgina. "Have *you* met Theo then?" she asked accusingly.

"It is not necessary for me to meet him, Sara. Frankly, I am surprised the Maitlands included him in Katherine's wedding party. I — *we* — have reached this decision on well-substantiated grounds. It isn't necessary to give you the reasons. But since it seems to have upset you so much, I can only remind you that I grew up in Beaufort, living many years in Charleston, and know that the Richardsons are not received in some of the best homes there. That is enough for me."

"But what has Theo done that is so terrible? I don't understand!"

"All right, Sara, if you insist!" Georgina lost her patience. "His family is declassé. His parents are . . . separated, if you must know. His father is a flagrant gambler, went through his own inheritance as well as his poor wife's fortune. His reputation is well known in Charleston. The family lives in a ramshackle plantation house on Sullivan's Island, never entertain, and are rarely invited anywhere. Anyone who associates with them socially would be tainted by these distasteful circumstances."

Sara's reaction was immediate.

"Why must Theo be blamed for what his

father has done or is? I know him and he is every inch a gentleman — a fine, agreeable, mannerly person I would be proud to have call on me!" Sara defended hotly.

At this, Mr. Leighton threw down his napkin. "That's enough, Sara. The matter is closed."

Frustrated, Sara rushed on heedlessly. "Please, Papa, meet him and decide for yourself. I know you would agree that a person should be judged on his own merits. I can't believe you would take this malicious gossip Georgina has repeated as fact —"

Mr. Leighton's fist came crashing down on the table, causing the crystal goblets to rattle, the silverware to shift. "Enough, Sara!" he roared. "I never heard such impertinence! No child of mine shall defy me. You'll do as you're told, miss, or I'll know the reason why!"

Lucie gave Sara a sharp little warning kick. When Sara glanced in her direction, she actually seemed to be cowering. Lucie hated scenes, feared her father's displeasure. At that moment something hardened in Sara. She would not give in. She would fight — for her freedom, and for Lucie's!

Georgina sat frozen, glaring at her, and Sara felt wild resentment race through her. But she willed herself to calm. Pushing back her chair, Sara asked her father, "May I be excused?"

"No, Miss Sara, you may not," came his quick angry reply. "You will sit there until the rest of us are finished, if you please."

The painful silence lengthened. The only sound was the scraping of silver on porcelain, the muted footsteps of Trent moving around the table refilling the water glasses. At last Mr. Leighton rose from his chair.

"You will apologize to your stepmother, Sara, and I hope there's an end to your insupportable behavior."

Sara never knew how she had obeyed her father and murmured the commanded apology. Dizzy as she was with anger, she was determined not to risk further punishment. Continuing to argue might result in bringing Georgina's retribution down upon her. She couldn't risk that — not if it meant being deprived of the rest of the wedding activities still to come . . . and Theo's presence.

As she left the dining room, head held high, the quotation "Love laughs at locksmiths" flashed through Sara's mind. *Georgina has met her match,* she thought.

Sara would not be defeated. She would find a way to be with Theo, even if it meant that eventually they would have to elope!

chapter 5

At the wedding rehearsal at the church, Sara had no opportunity to speak with Theo, and afterwards they were seated in different carriages on their way to the Maitland home for the rehearsal dinner.

She was still stinging from the scene with her father and Georgina the day before. It had taken all her will power not to aggravate the situation further. Outwardly resigned, Sara was seething. Opposition always succeeded in making her more determined. She began to plot several extravagant schemes to outwit her stepmother's arbitrary decision not to receive Theo. Although Sara railed against Georgina's influence on her father, she knew she was helpless to sway him now.

If anything, their position excited Sara's recklessness, enhanced Theo's desirability, increased her romantic fantasy. Star-crossed lovers they might be, but together they would find a way. Theo loved her.

Hadn't he said so in his letters? And she loved him. She dreamed of the drama of an elopement, the shock waves it would send through Savannah society. That would show Georgina!

When the bridesmaids reached the Maitlands' home, Sara found a chance to slip away. The bevy of girls went upstairs to freshen up. As soon as she could without drawing attention to herself, Sara went downstairs in search of Theo, leaving the others crowding in front of the mirrors to primp, powder, and fuss with hairdos.

Defiantly she had devised a plan for meeting Theo secretly. Tomorrow, accompanied by Mammy June, she had the final fitting of her bridesmaid's gown. Theo could meet her in one of Savannah's secluded squares in the salon. There, unseen, unchaperoned, they could at last talk freely and privately. Oh, how she longed for that moment!

Once downstairs, Sara paused. Hearing the sound of men's voices and laughter coming from one of the twin parlors, she moved closer. Her surreptitious peek told her that the male members of the wedding party were enjoying a jovial libation before joining the ladies. But Theo was not among them. Where could he be?

Checking the other parlor, she found the musicians arranging their instruments and music stands on a raised platform at one end of the room. The doors at the other end opened into the dining room, where the house servants were arranging a huge silver punchbowl and cups on a table covered with a lace tablecloth.

"Miss Leighton!" drawled a deep voice from behind her. Startled, Sara whirled around and pitched forward, very nearly into the arms of Clayborn Montrose.

"What luck!" he said, steadying her before reluctantly withdrawing his arm. His eyes moved over her with undisguised pleasure. "I had hoped I would have this privilege. And here it is. May I get you some punch?" he asked, unaware of her bitter disappointment that he was not Theo.

All Sara could do was accept. Having placed herself in the awkward situation of being downstairs alone, the only thing to do was carry it off with as much grace as possible.

Clayborn offered his arm and Sara took it, allowing herself to be led over to one of the gilded chairs set in conversational semicircles about the large room. She seated herself and Clay went to get their refreshment. He was back in a moment, brandishing two punch cups and a smug smile.

"This punch is famous, I'm told by Fax, always served in Savannah on festive occasions," Clayborn said as he handed her a cup. "The original recipe is a secret, but over the years the ingredients have become a matter of common knowledge, at least among some southern hosts," he told her, taking a seat beside her. He lifted his cup in a toast, eyes twinkling, then lowered his voice conspiratorially, "As a matter of fact, I'm one of the privileged few who know what is in it!"

Distracted as she was, Sara was schooled in the social etiquette of pretending an interest she did not feel. "And pray tell, what are those mysterious ingredients, Mr. Montrose?"

Clayborn, smiling with satisfaction that he had caught her attention, said, "It seems the members of the Chatham Artillery, one of the oldest military organizations in existence before 1775, were preparing to entertain President James Monroe, on his way to Savannah for the gala launching of the S.S. *Savannah* on its historic Atlantic voyage. They wanted something very special to serve the chief executive of the United States. So this beverage was created." Clay's eyes sparkled mischievously. "Fax warned me it's very potent!"

"Then I shall have to be careful not to let it go to my head, shan't I?" Sara laughed.

"Personally, *I* need nothing more than your company, Miss Leighton, to feel quite dizzy and disoriented."

Sara gave him a questioning look, surprised that the bantering tone was gone. He was really quite serious.

Her expression must have revealed how much he had disconcerted her. As if anxious to explain, Clay rushed on, "I apologize for my frankness. I realize we are practically strangers. It is my misfortune, but not my fault, that I am unknown to you. I also understand that my behavior is completely against all accepted rules of protocol. But my justification is time. Or I should say lack of it. You see, Miss Leighton — *Sara* — may I call you Sara? — after the wedding I return immediately to Virginia to make preparations to leave for Europe. I will be out of the country for several months on my grand tour, a graduation present from my foster-mother, my Aunt Avril. If I don't speak now, something may happen in the meantime. You might even forget we ever met —"

Completely taken aback by this ardent declaration, Sara unfurled her little fan and began to flutter it briskly. She was accustomed to the light patter, the compliments and flattery, the pat phrases used in most social exchange. But this was something different altogether. She remained speechless as Clay continued earnestly.

"I could not take my eyes off you in church this evening. You were so lovely with the candlelight on your face — more beautiful than any of the other bridesmaids, or even the bride herself."

"Mr. Montrose, I must protest —" Sara interrupted him. "I cannot allow you to run on so! You are making me extremely uncomfortable. I am shocked that you should have been so frivolously distracted during such a solemn occasion as the rehearsal. And in all places, one where religious services are conducted!"

Of course, Sara was not as shocked as she pretended. She was, in fact, flattered that he thought her prettier than the serenely beautiful Katherine! Immediately her conscience pinched her for her duplicity.

"Then I doubly apologize if I have offended you." Clay seemed abject. "But I cannot deny my heart nor recant my true feelings."

To Sara's immense relief there was suddenly a flurry of activity, the sound of voices as the rest of the company began flowing into the room.

"If I felt I had reason to hope, I would come back to Savannah as soon as I returned from Europe." He took her free hand and covered it with his. "Please, Sara, please give me that hope."

"Mr. Montrose!" she remonstrated, tugging her hand gently away. "You forget yourself! You were correct in the first place. We have never even been properly introduced, you have never met my parents, nor called at my home. It is only due to our both being in this wedding that we even met . . . mere chance —"

"*Chance?* I would like to think it was a great deal more than that, Sara."

She could think of nothing more to say.

Over Clay's shoulder she saw Theo enter the room. She had to get to him before anything interfered. At once Sara got to her feet.

"You must excuse me," she murmured.

"May I be your partner at supper?" Clay asked.

She shook her head, her eyes following Theo as he stopped to speak to Katherine and Douglas Cameron.

"I'm sorry, I promised —"

"Then, may I have the first dance after?"

Eager to be away, Sara agreed. "Yes, I suppose so."

She tried to make her way across the room toward Theo, but two bridesmaids halted her to admire her dress. Just at that moment, a pretty blonde joined them. Though Sara did not know her, she assumed she was one of many out-of-town guests come for the wedding. There was no way Sara could break away without appearing rude.

With a simpering giggle, the blonde asked in a stage whisper, "Oh, do tell me, before he gets away. Who is that devastatingly handsome gentleman with the dark curly hair talking with Katherine?"

Sara did not need to look. She knew the gentleman in question.

"That's Theo Richardson," one of the other bridesmaids replied.

"Oh, isn't he adorable?" the blonde sighed.

"Well, don't get any ideas," retorted her friend. "He's spoken for."

Sara stiffened. How could anyone possibly have guessed about her romance with Theo?

"What do you mean?" came the blonde's plaintive voice.

"Surely you knew. It was announced in the Charleston paper last week. He and Evangeline Archer are engaged."

chapter 6

Sara felt shock jolt through her body, followed by a sickening chill. Numbed, she heard with growing disbelief the rest of the conversation between the other girls.

"The Archers are old-family Charlestonians, you know."

"They have a shipbuilding firm."

"A gorgeous home on the Battery."

"And a plantation on the Island."

"Of course, Evangeline —" began one of them.

"But she *is* real sweet —"

"She was at the Academe last year."

"But who would ever have thought? I mean, Evangeline?"

Suddenly Sara could listen no more. She felt hot, faint, and clenched her hands together, willing herself to control the mounting tide of pain threatening to engulf her. Fighting the urge to scream, she looked straight ahead and into Theo's eyes. The impact of that glance struck her like a blow to her chest, and she gasped. *How could he?*

They stared at each other, motionless. Everything seemed to recede — the voices, the laughter, the music softly playing in the background. Then Sara turned away.

Blindly, she hurried toward the French windows opening onto the veranda. Once outside, she took a deep breath, drawing the cool night air into bursting lungs. Wanting only to escape, she began to run, the gravel stone path cutting into the thin soles of her satin slippers.

Can it be true? But how? The letters Theo wrote . . . He said he loved me! The tormenting thoughts clutched at her brain, driving her on. Though it had been weeks since she had heard from him, she *knew* he loved her. It had been in his eyes, in his voice just the other night, in his kiss. It couldn't be true!

Breathless, she stopped her frantic flight and stumbled over to a large oak tree. Leaning against it, she put out her hands, indifferent to the rough bark through the fragile lace of her mitts.

The whisper of the evening breeze cooled her hot cheeks, but now the choking sobs began. *Theo, Theo, how could you be so false?* her breaking heart demanded. Only a few hours ago she had been sure he loved her, was as eager to see her as she had been to be with him. How could she have been so deluded? so wrong? Oh, the humiliation of it!

And who was Evangeline Archer? They had said she was at the Academe last year. But so was Lucie. Surely Lucie would have known about the romance. And Lucie would not have kept such a relationship from her, would she?

Sara drew a long, painful breath. She could hear music floating out through the long windows of the house. She must go back in. But how could she? How could she face anyone after this? How could she bear to see Theo now that she knew the truth?

"Sara."

At the sound of that mellow, once-beloved voice with its distinctive Low Country accent, Sara froze, unable to move nor speak.

"Sara." She could tell he was directly behind her now, only a few feet away.

He spoke her name a third time, tenderly, caressingly. Then she felt his hand on her arm.

"Don't!" She shook it off and moved away.

"Sara, please. I've been waiting for this chance to be alone with you —"

She twirled about, her taffeta skirts rustling in the quietness of the garden. "Oh, really! Have you now? Waiting for what, Theo? Enough time to muster the courage to tell me of your engagement? Well, it was time wasted. I already know." Her voice was steely, hard, almost unrecognizable, even to herself.

His face, illuminated by the moonlight, looked anguished. "Sara, I wanted to see you in person, tell you. I . . . I didn't want to write you —"

"Why not?" Her laugh was mirthless. "You found it easy enough to write other things. And I quote, 'My dearest, how I long to see you. The days cannot pass swiftly enough until I am with you again . . .' It would have been simple enough, I should think. Just a few lines: 'By the way, Sara, I am planning to marry someone else.' But then, it seems you are singularly lacking in courage, Theo," she said with contempt. "I wonder you find it now. Your courtship with Miss Evangeline Archer must have been going on all the time you were telling me how much you loved *me!* How base can you be?"

"Sara, I beg you to hear me out."

"What is there to say? People fall in and out of love all the time. Easily. I've done it myself. I daresay I'll do it again." Sara flourished her fan and shrugged.

"Sara —" Theo's voice shook with emotion. "Sara, please don't wound me more. I know my faults, my lack of courage, if you will, better than anyone. If you will only hear me out, perhaps you will understand. For the sake of what we have meant to each other, please give me a chance to explain."

Sara's hurt was too raw for reply. Taking her silence for assent, Theo reached for her hand and drew her back to the bench circling the oak tree, and they sat down together.

"Sara, I have told you about my family situation. Honestly. The disgrace my father has brought upon us all. Two months ago he died — no need to tell you how — accidentally or by his own hand, no one is sure. It was left to me, the only son . . . to go through his papers." Theo paused to regain his composure. "Debt piled upon debt . . . and no money . . . to pay any of them." He stood and paced in front of her. "Vance Archer has been a friend of my mother's family for years. Of my father as well, though in recent years he had become disgusted with . . . well, the things my father did. Still, Mr. Archer came to me and offered to clear up all my father's affairs. Can you imagine what this meant, Sara? To my mother, to me, to my sisters?"

Again Theo paused, struggling with his emotions. "He also offered me a job as a designer in his shipbuilding firm, completely overlooking my lack of qualifications. He just took me on so that I could provide for my mother and sisters."

"Don't tell me you are marrying his daughter out of gratitude to her father?" Sara demanded.

"Sara, I do owe Mr. Archer . . . everything."

"Not your life, surely?"

There was another long pause. Theo dropped back onto the bench and took both Sara's hands in his. Looking directly into her eyes, shadowed by the branches of the overhanging tree, he spoke firmly. "I have known Evangeline since childhood. She is gentle, kind, and good, Sara. She loves me. And I love her. . . . And, yes, we are to be married."

Sara pulled her hands away and stood up. "I can't believe you would be so mercenary as to marry someone because her father offers you a position —"

Theo sighed. Getting to his feet, he threw out his hands in a gesture of helplessness.

"Sara, don't you realize that *your* father would never have consented to our being engaged, would never have allowed his daughter to marry a man with my background, my family history, and no prospects? What would I have to offer someone like you?"

"Oh, Theo, do you think I care about that? That's not important. If we love each other —" she exclaimed, hope rising in her again. "Besides, I know you *do* love me, no matter what you say! And I love you! We could run away and be married. Then everyone would have to accept it!"

Impulsively Sara took a step toward him. In another moment she flung her arms around his neck, her fingers tangling in the silky curls at the nape of his neck.

She heard Theo suppress a moan as his arms tightened around her. "No, Sara, no. Don't make it harder for both of us." She felt his breath warm against her cheek. "Sara, darling, we mustn't —"

"Oh, Theo, why not?" Sara cried. "I don't care about anything but us!"

There was a moment's hesitation, and then he kissed her. Sara's lips, soft and pliant beneath his, responded with all the eager urgency of her passionate heart.

Then, slowly, gently he pushed her away.

Framing her face in both hands, he looked down at her. "Sara, dearest, there is no going back. I can't change things. I am already committed. It's too late —"

"No!" A sob caught in her throat. "No, it isn't!"

But Theo put his fingers over her lips, stopping her words. He shook his head. "Sara, everything is settled. I have already taken a position in Mr. Archer's firm, my father's debts are paid, my engagement to Evangeline has been announced, the wedding date is set —"

Sara's body went rigid. She stared at him for a full minute, then she stepped back and brought her small, ivory fan up and slammed it across his cheek.

"Coward!" she hissed. "You are despicable!"

Theo flinched. Instinctively, his hand went to his cheek. "Yes, Sara, I suppose you have a right to call me that."

Stunned by her own action, Sara stood like a statue. Though she heard the music wafting through the garden, smelled the scent of roses, saw the Spanish moss swaying overhead, nothing penetrated. All she could feel was a strange, all-absorbing grief, an overwhelming loss.

Stiffly, she turned and moved woodenly

back toward the house. Theo's voice followed her.

"Sara, I hope someday you can find it in your heart to forgive me — perhaps even to understand."

She did not reply, nor did she look back to see Theo, slumped against the tree.

Raw with hurt and anger, Sara stood for a minute on the veranda, her blood burning her cheeks to flame, her heart beating in her ears like a metronome at "allegro." She must get control of herself before returning to the party. No one must suspect anything was wrong. Pride was Sara's only weapon against her wounded spirit, and she gathered it around her like a tattered garment. It was all she had left.

Drawing a deep breath, she willed herself to smile, set her shoulders and reentered the house. She saw Clayborn Montrose's relieved expression as he started across the room to claim her for the dance she had promised him. With feverish gaiety Sara flung herself back into the party.

Somehow — she never knew how — Sara got through that evening. Moving from partner to partner, she danced, smiled, made light conversation, even laughed. No one would have guessed that under the bright smile, the gaiety, was heartbreak.

Only Sara knew that lodged deep within was an unfathomable ache and that after this night, nothing would ever be the same for her again.

chapter 7

At the end of the evening, two of the Maitland carriages drew up in front of the house to take the Savannah bridesmaids home. Each group of six was accompanied by two of Douglas Cameron's groomsmen, who gallantly escorted them to their own door.

To Sara's great relief, Theo was not asked to be one of the escorts.

All the way over to the Leightons' house, she kept up the lighthearted patter expected of her. At her door she bade her escorts good night with her usual coquetry. Maintaining this façade was only possible by exercising her iron will over her breaking heart.

Trent, who had been drowsing in a chair in the hall awaiting his young mistress's return, opened the front door for her. Sara picked up the lamp left burning for her on the hall table, and started for the stairs.

At the bottom of the staircase, she kicked off her slippers. As she started up, she discarded her evening cloak. It fell in a shimmer of taffeta and lace on the steps behind, as did the mask she had worn for the last few hours.

The strain of the evening had given her a throbbing head, and she rubbed her forehead absently. Tears that had been forced back all evening trickled down her cheeks. By the time she reached the upper hall and started toward her sister's bedroom, they were flowing, unchecked.

She flung open Lucie's door and in a few quick steps was beside her bed. Holding the lamp high, Sara ripped off the quilt with her other hand and began shaking her sleeping sister.

"Why didn't you tell me?" she demanded. "Why didn't you tell me about Theo Richardson and Evangeline Archer?"

Roused so roughly out of a sound sleep, Lucie stared up at her sister blankly. Then she sat up, blinking, trying to make sense of what Sara was saying.

"Tell you what? I don't know what you're talking about, Sara!" she protested, rubbing her eyes.

"Don't you dare lie to me, Lucie! Don't tell me you didn't know Theo was coming to see her on Visitors' Day at the Academe! *Courting* her! How could you let me walk into that . . . that awful situation not knowing?"

"But, Sara, I didn't know! I *don't* know!" Lucie whimpered. "I promise you I don't know anything about it!" Lucie's eyes were wide, and Sara saw her innocence.

Suddenly the fury drained away. Only the terrible, aching pain remained. She set the lamp on the table beside the bed and sank down beside Lucie on the feather mattress.

"You *did* know, *do* know Evangeline Archer though, don't you, Lucie?" prodded Sara. "She was at the Academy last year."

Lucie's brow furrowed with the effort of remembering. "Well, yes, sort of, Sara. But she was a 'special student' — you know, the ones who don't attend all the regular classes or participate in every activity. She lived in Charleston and went home on weekends so I never saw Theo come on Visitors' Day. Cross my heart, Sara!" Lucie insisted earnestly.

"Can you remember anything about her?" Sara was adamant in her questioning. "What did she look like? Was she pretty? Tell me everything you can think of."

Lucie's small, kitten face wrinkled. "She was rather plain, I think," she said, "but with a sweet expression. Quite shy, I believe. She was a music student, played the harp. Very well, too. She played for some of Madame's concerts for parents. You remember those, don't you?"

"Yes, yes!" Sara said impatiently. "But I want to hear about *her*, about Evangeline."

"She always wore beautiful clothes, Sara. Her family is very rich, people said. But then, it didn't help much, poor thing, because of her problem."

"Problem? What do you mean, problem?"

"Well, she limps terribly, Sara. One leg is shorter than the other. They say it happened when she was a baby, some sort of accident — a nurse dropped her, or something — and one leg never grew properly. So, it makes her walk with an awkward sort of gait —"

Sara seemed to have turned to stone. She sat absolutely immobile, drained of color.

"Sara, Sara, what is it?" Lucie asked in a whisper. She reached out and took one of her sister's hands. It was icy cold.

Sara did not answer. Her mind was centered on the tragic truth behind Theo's betrayal. Pity. He had married a crippled girl out of pity. Did Evangeline know? She must have guessed. A man as handsome and charming as Theo tying himself to a woman no other man would have! She *must* know.

For a minute Sara closed her eyes. She

thought of Theo on the dance floor, so graceful and accomplished, spinning his partner to every kind of music — the schottische, the polka, the new waltz. Was Theo resigned to a life without music and dancing? Married to a woman who could never dance with him, or ride horseback, or even stroll on his arm? What a dreadful fate.

"Sara." Lucie plucked at Sara's sleeve, her voice cautious. "What happened to-night to make you so angry, so unhappy?"

Slowly Sara brought her thoughts back to the painful present. "Theo is engaged to be married, Lucie. To Evangeline Archer."

Lucie drew in her breath, eyes wide with disbelief. "No!"

Sara nodded. "I wish it weren't true, but it is. He told me himself."

"Oh, Sara, I'm so sorry!" wailed Lucie, putting her arms around her sister.

"It's not your fault." Sara patted her as the two clung together. "I blame myself for being fool enough to trust him. No wonder he insisted we keep our romance a secret. All the time he was writing love letters to me, he must have been seeing her — must have *known* that he —" Sara began to cry, and her tears of self-pity mingled with Lucie's sympathetic ones.

Finally the sobs lessened. Sara dried her

eyes, took a tiny handkerchief out of her reticule, and blew her nose. "Well, anyway, this has taught me a hard lesson I hope I'll never forget, Lucie."

Lucie looked at Sara's beautiful face, blotched with crying, her eyelids red and swollen, and she noticed something she had never seen there before. The soft mouth had hardened visibly, and there was a new firmness about her jaw.

"At least no one but you will ever know. Not by a single word or gesture will I let anyone know how hurt I am. I can act, Lucie. Remember how good I was in the part of Portia when we put on *The Merchant of Venice* at the Academe? Well, for the rest of the wedding week, I'll have to be an actress. Theo will never suspect that I even *care!*" She lifted her chin defiantly.

"Oh, Sara, you're so brave! I don't think I could be in the wedding party. I couldn't bear *seeing* him!"

Sara turned to her sister, eyes flashing. "No, Lucie! It is *he* who should dread seeing *me!*" she declared. "I have nothing to be ashamed of!"

But, of course, she had, Sara reminded herself guiltily. She had been party to a deception, had carried on a secret romance, involving a friend in the conspiracy. Now she was paying a heavy price for what she had done. All of it — a year of clandestine meetings, stolen kisses, evasive tactics. In fact, a *year* of lies. Still, she *was* being punished for her sins, she thought.

Rising, she bent over and kissed Lucie's cheek. "I'm sorry I woke you. I was angry and upset. Go back to sleep now. I'll be all right."

Mammy June, who had always slept on a cot at the foot of Sara's bed when her "young missy" went out for the evening, was sleeping heavily when Sara slipped into her own bedroom. She moved about quietly, not wanting to arouse the old woman nor subject herself to more questions.

Sara undressed quickly and got into bed. She didn't fall asleep right away, however. There was too much to think about, too many plans to make. The rest of her life, actually!

Tonight she had been shown the ugliness of deceit. She vowed never to employ it again.

Lying awake, Sara also determined never to be so vulnerable again. But how was she going to get through the rest of the wedding week? It would take all her will power and strength.

She shrank from an imagined encounter with Theo the next day. But her new resolve fueled her determination. She would get through it by playing a part. She would play the role of bridesmaid to perfection, participating in an elaborate pageant, Katherine's wedding.

Theo was just another player, she told herself. But at the thought, Sara was biting her lower lip, her sharp little teeth cutting into the soft flesh, lest she cry out his name.

Weeks later, whenever Sara recalled the wedding, it was through a merciful fog. She had moved through the party given by the bridesmaids for Katherine in a kind of suspended trance, laughing with the rest over the silly gifts, exchanging bits of gossip and compliments, and engaging in frivolous conversation.

Then the wedding day dawned. The historic church, from whose pulpit both the illustrious John Wesley and George Whitfield had preached, was filled with flowers and elegantly dressed guests on that warm summer afternoon. Garlands draped the pews, baskets of lilies, heliotrope, and roses graced the aisles down which the dozen bridesmaids preceded the bride.

Gowned in ruffled dresses in rainbow hues, they came two-by-two, carrying bouquets of garden flowers.

Sara was one of a duo in blue. Around her neck was Katherine's keepsake gift to her attendants — a delicate gold chain from which hung a pearl cross centered with each girl's birthstone.

It should have been a happy day. But, for Sara, it was the hardest day of her life. The ceremony itself was torture — trying not to hear the meaningful words, avoiding even the slightest chance of meeting Theo's gaze —

The reception was even more difficult, as it lasted long into the afternoon hours and was held in the most festive atmosphere. Only Clayborn Montrose's flattering attention saved Sara from complete desolation in spite of her determination to hide her feelings. Having appointed himself her escort for the afternoon, his obvious admiration was a balm to her bruised pride.

Clayborn made a great point of introducing her to his "foster mother," Avril Montrose, a lady of great dignity and charm, who had traveled all the way from her home in Virginia to attend the wedding.

"Aunt Avril has just come out of formal mourning for my Uncle Graham," Clay explained. "In fact, this is the first social occasion she has attended since his death. Theirs was a real love story, very romantic.

I'd like to tell you about it sometime."

Sara managed a smile. The very last thing she wanted to hear was a "romantic love story."

It was Clay, however, who made the whole long day endurable. Clay, with his thoughtfulness, his attentiveness, his consideration. He seemed to know just when to make a humorous remark or observation and when to remain quiet.

For Sara, under the surface of indifference, the face and form of Theo Richardson seemed to float in and out, hover close, then disappear. It was as if they were doing some intricate dance, circling each other, advancing and retreating, swinging to and fro in an odd sort of duet whose steps neither had quite mastered.

Somehow, I survived, Sara thought with some surprise as the reception at last drew to a close. *Soon I can go home.*

Everyone gathered in the front hall as the newly married couple stood ready to rush down the steps and outside to their waiting carriage. But first there was a traditional ritual to perform.

Sara was only vaguely aware of the flurry of activity, playful shouting of good wishes, and laughter surrounding her as Katherine poised on the landing of the stairs to toss her bridal bouquet. Then it came flying through the air.

No one was more surprised than Sara herself when she found it in her own outstretched hands!

Montclair
Spring 1831

chapter 8

The late spring morning was cool, misted with the soft rain that had fallen earlier, as Clayborn Montrose turned his mount in at the gate and started up the tree-lined drive toward Montclair.

Elm trees, bare when he left in the fall for his European tour, were now in full foliage. The woods bordering the lawn were dotted pink and white with flowering dogwood. All along the drive rosy azaleas, red and pink rhododendron, and pale lavender spears of lilacs tossed their blooms in the light breeze. In the orchard, frothy lace blossoms adorned the peach and apple trees, their sweetness perfuming the air.

Clay felt that combination of pride and affection swell in his chest the nearer he came to the place he had called home since he was eleven years old. He had come here as an orphan; he was returning now as son and heir.

From Williamsburg, after arriving from Norfolk where his ship had docked, Clay had sent word to his foster mother, that after he had paid his respects to the Barnwell kin here, he would be home.

If he knew Aunt Avril, Clay smiled, she had probably been up since dawn preparing for his homecoming. They were unusually close, with many things bonding them to each other. The tragic childhood experience of losing both parents at a tender age was the common link between them. That initial empathy became mutual trust and devotion that had deepened with each year. Besides that was the strong love they shared for Avril's husband, Graham, who had once been her guardian as well as Clay's.

Avril was more than a mother to him. She was friend, advisor, champion, and mentor. She had listened to his problems, encouraged his dreams, strengthened his faith.

He was as eager to see her as she was anxiously awaiting their reunion after the long months of separation.

That evening Avril served dinner at the small table in the bow window of the dining room overlooking the sweeping lawns. In the pre-twilight they could still see the rim of the river glistening in the last rays of sun.

"I cannot begin to tell you how much I have missed you, darling boy, and how glad I am to have you home." Avril reached across the table to press Clayborn's hand. "With the whole long summer ahead of us to enjoy! I have so many plans, so many ideas, so many things I want to discuss with you. It will be a great relief to me to turn some of this over to you, Clay."

Since Graham's death Avril had managed the Montclair plantation with the help of Jacob Neal, their longtime overseer, as well as by relying on the advice of Marshall Cameron, her close friend and owner of the neighboring plantation, Cameron Hall.

"I'll give you a week or so to visit your friends and relax before I heap the whole burden on you, though. So don't look so worried!" she admonished him, laughing.

"That's the least of my concerns, Aunt Avril," Clay replied. "I've always known I'd take over at Montclair someday, and I want to. You've carried the full weight long enough. It's just that there's something else I have to do first."

"Oh? What is that?"

"I'm not sure you'll approve," he said slowly, picking up his fork and tracing a design on the linen tablecloth.

A small frown puckered Avril's brow.

"Clay, dear, you are a grown man, twenty-one. You no longer need my approval," she reminded him. Then, probing subtly, she added, "But knowing what a fine person you are and that you have always been such a joy and comfort to me, I cannot imagine your doing anything I would *not* approve of."

He lifted his head from the scroll he had outlined and looked directly into his aunt's curious eyes.

"I want to go to Savannah."

"Savannah?" Avril echoed. "*Why* Savannah?"

"Maybe I should have said I want to go see someone who lives in Savannah."

"And who is that, darling? Have you forgotten that the Pierces go to their mountain home to escape the heat from the first of May through September?"

"No, Aunt Avril, it isn't Fax Pierce I want to see. It's a young lady."

"Oh! Well, I see." Avril nodded. "Someone you met at Doug's wedding?"

"Yes, how did you guess?"

"That wasn't difficult since Savannah was the last place we visited before you left for Europe." Avril shrugged. "And who is this lucky young lady who tempts you to take another long trip when you have just come home?"

"You met her at the reception. I introduced you to her. She was one of Katherine's bridesmaids. Her name is Sara Leighton."

"Sara Leighton?" Avril repeated, raising her eyebrows.

"Yes, Aunt Avril. She is extraordinarily beautiful, don't you remember? She was wearing blue the color of her eyes, and her smile —" As if at a loss for words, Clay halted. Then, leaning forward eagerly, he asked, "Surely you remember *Sara?*"

"Let me see —" Avril seemed to be trying to concentrate. "Of course, *all* the young ladies were lovely —"

"Yes, yes, but Sara was the loveliest." Clay got to his feet as if his excitement was too much to contain. "Oh, Aunt Avril, I adore her! I want to ask her to marry me. That's why I must go to Savannah right away."

"But, darling, you haven't seen her in almost a year. Have you considered that such a belle as she might have become engaged or even married to someone else by now?"

"No! No, she hasn't. We've been corresponding, Aunt Avril. I've written to her from all over Europe, and she replied. Oh, not so often as I. But I know she is still free. I have told her I'd come as soon as I got back. If she is willing, I plan to ask her father's permission." Clay stopped pacing and spun around to face his aunt. "So, what do you think?"

Avril hesitated. "Well, darling, I must admit I *have* heard of Sara. When I was in Savannah for the wedding, you know Marshall, Becky, and I stayed with Alvena Maitland's sister. Katherine's aunt is, I'm afraid, a great gossip. And I regret to tell you Sara was discussed."

"Yes? Well, what was said?"

"I don't like to repeat unpleasant things, Clay. But in this case, since you are seriously considering proposing to her, I think I should tell you. Sara was in the center of a recent scandal. A duel, which was fortunately averted. Still, it seems she was the cause —"

"Probably vicious lies," commented Clay firmly. "Anyone as beautiful and popular as Sara is bound to create jealousy. I don't care, Aunt Avril. I love her."

"And does she return your love?"

"She has not discouraged me," Clay hedged. "We spent the whole reception together and when we parted, I asked her if she would allow me to write, and call upon her when I returned. She said that would make her very happy." He clapped his hands together as if that settled it.

"But calling on a young lady is quite different from proposing marriage, Clay," Avril cautioned.

"In my letters I have hinted broadly as to what I have in mind when I come to Savannah. I think she has an idea of my intentions. In fact, in the last letter I received before sailing for home, she wrote she was looking forward to my visit." Clay's happiness was so evident that Avril had not the heart to tell him the way her Savannah hostess had described Miss Sara Leighton.

"Sara Leighton is as reckless on horseback as she is graceful in the ballroom, as fond of her pets as she is heartless to suitors she disdains."

Such a description did not fit the ideal Avril had always held for her adopted son's bride nor her hope for a possible future mistress of Montclair. But Avril was wise enough to keep her misgivings about Clay's trip to herself, and within a fortnight he set out for Savannah.

Two days later Logan Cameron rode over from Cameron Hall. Since he had always considered Montclair a second home to which he needed no invitation, he strode into the house as if he lived there and went in search of Avril.

Finding her at the desk in the plantation office off the library, he greeted her with the familiarity of long friendship. "Good afternoon, ma'am. I've come to welcome the prodigal home. Where is he?"

Avril looked up from the ledgers she was working on, saw Logan leaning against the doorframe, and sighed. "Not here."

"Not here? Mama told me he just got home ten days ago!"

"Gone again."

"Gone where?" Logan sounded astonished.

"Savannah."

"Savannah?"

"Oh, Logan, *must* you repeat everything I say?" asked Avril in exasperation, flinging down her pen. Then she gave him a rueful smile. "Forgive me, dear friend. I'm feeling upset, I'm afraid. Too long at these figures, I suspect. Let's go and have some refreshment and I'll tell you all about it."

She came from around the desk, putting aside unpleasantries. "It's good to see you, Logan. You've been gone a long while. Where were you this time?"

"New Orleans. Some estate business. One of father's old clients," he told her, tucking her arm through his as they made their way back through the high-ceilinged house.

With Hugh Cameron less inclined to travel as he grew older, Logan was taking over more and more of the judge's law practice.

When they were seated in comfortable rush rockers on the shady side of the veranda, sipping minted iced tea, Avril confided in her longtime friend. "Clay has gone to propose marriage to someone I am afraid cannot possibly make him happy."

"And who is that? And how can you be so sure she can't make him happy?"

"Oh, Logan, you're always so logical," Avril accused. "Wanting all the facts. A typical lawyer!"

Briefly she told him what she knew of Sara Leighton.

"And Clayborn loves her?"

"Madly." Avril sighed deeply. "Although I can't account for it. They only met at Doug Cameron's wedding and could scarcely know each other!"

Logan rose and walked over to the porch railing. Leaning on it with his hands, he gazed out toward the orchards and past to the woods. "Then there's nothing you can do about it."

"If only —" began Avril.

"If only Clay had fallen in love with someone you knew and approved of, someone right for him?" Logan finished the sentence for her. He turned, regarding Avril thoughtfully.

She reached for her glass and took a sip, returning his appraisal over its rim.

Logan had always been handsome, the best looking of the two Cameron boys, she thought. But now his features were mature, stamped with a sophistication born of experience and responsibility. He was looking at her now with that amused irony she recognized from earlier days.

"You know me too well," she said.

"Fairy-tale endings. You always wanted fairy-tale endings, Avril," Logan remarked. "Life doesn't always oblige."

"I got mine!" she reminded him.

Logan did not comment right away. He shrugged. "Perhaps. But some of us fall in love with the wrong person. That is, someone who is either wrong or one who doesn't love us in return."

"I trust Clayborn," Avril said firmly. "He has good judgment. Maybe when he sees Sara again, spends more time with her, he'll realize —"

"Love has nothing to do with good judgment. It's a kind of insanity!" declared

Logan. "No conscientious lawyer would allow his client to sign a binding agreement in the state of mind most people are in when about to commit themselves to marriage."

Avril's eyes filled with merriment. "Oh, Logan, you're good for me! You make me laugh! I wish you'd open your own law office in Mayfield and not travel so much, or at least come home to Cameron Hall more often!"

"I cannot endure all the domestic bliss that abounds there these days," he retorted, eyes twinkling mischievously. "Doug and his bride are still honeymooners, and, for that matter, Marshall and Becky are not much past that themselves. And as for the three younger children — especially the little girls!" Logan raised both hands in mock horror. "Those two are more rambunctious than Marshall and I ever were! Becky's going to have her hands full trying to turn those hoydens into young ladies."

Avril laughed again and realized it had been a long time since she had. She was sorry when Logan rose from his chair.

"Well, I better be on my way," he said. "I'm disappointed not to have seen Clay. I was anxious to hear his impressions of his European travels."

"He should be back at the end of the

month, Logan. Maybe sooner, if he doesn't get the answer he's hoping for." Avril walked with him to the front of the porch. One of the little boys from the quarters was sitting on the grass beside Logan's gelding, holding the reins while the horse grazed. "You'll still be here then, won't you?"

"I think so." He started down the steps. "In the meantime, why don't you and I go riding some morning?" Looking back over his shoulder, he said, "Like the old days."

"I'd like that!" exclaimed Avril happily.

"Good! Why not tomorrow? Eight o'clock?"

"Fine," she agreed. "I'll be ready."

As Avril stood watching Logan ride down the drive and out of sight, she suddenly knew how much she had missed him. Especially in these last three lonely years of widowhood. Logan, who had been her childhood playmate, the companion of her youth, her confidant and friend. As she went back inside, Avril was smiling — she was looking forward to tomorrow.

Even though she knew Logan was right when he said there was nothing she could do about Clay's infatuation with Sara Leighton, Avril relied on that which had always given her comfort and guidance.

That night she knelt at her bedroom window, looking out on the beauty that was Montclair by moonlight, and prayed for the young man who was as dear to her as any child of her own could be. Having known the perfect joy of a good marriage, where love is given and returned in full measure, she asked that her son be granted the same. But before she got up from her knees, Avril also prayed for the girl he loved so blindly.

Part II

Savannah

Summer 1831

chapter 9

"I declare, Leonard! I am completely baffled by Sara's behavior!" Georgina complained to her husband as they sat at breakfast one morning. "I can't imagine what ails the girl. Last year we could not curtail her activities, and now she doesn't want to go anywhere or see anyone." She frowned as if just making a fresh discovery. "Sara must be engaged and married before we can launch Lucie, you know. And Lucie will soon be sixteen and graduating school in June. Then what shall we do?"

Frowning, Leonard spooned more sugar into his coffee and stirred without reply. He wished Georgina would not annoy him with this sort of nonsense. He did not want to start his day hearing that Sara was being difficult again!

Clearing his throat, he said placatingly, "I wouldn't fret, my dear. Perhaps it's just a phase."

"But it's gone on for months, Leonard!"

protested Georgina. "Ever since Katherine Maitland's wedding, as a matter of fact. I don't understand it."

"Well, who can understand Sara?" he asked, irritated to have his breakfast spoiled by such trivial feminine matters.

"But, Leonard, I want to plan Lucie's debut for the Christmas holidays, and if Sara won't cooperate —"

Pulling out his watch on its heavy gold chain, Leonard consulted it and said, "Well, I must be off to the Exchange, my dear. Can't we postpone this decision about parties until some better time?"

Georgina looked injured, and he groaned inwardly. Going around the table, he dropped a light kiss on her cheek. At the very same moment, Sara, dressed in a forest green riding habit, appeared at the dining room door.

"Good morning, Papa. Good morning, Stepmama," Sara greeted them as she took her place at the table.

"Nice ride, Sara?" Leonard asked, thinking how splendid his eldest daughter looked, her vivid coloring enhanced by her exercise in the bracing air.

"Wonderful!" She held out her cup for Georgina to fill it with coffee.

"Riding alone seems to be the only outing

you enjoy these days, Sara," Georgina remarked insinuatingly.

Sara gave her stepmother a cool glance and took a sip of coffee.

Sensing the beginning of the familiar tug of wills between his wife and daughter, Leonard started for the door. "Goodbye, my dears. See you at noon," he said, and walked briskly out into the hall, passing Trent, the butler bringing in the morning mail on a small silver tray, which he placed before Georgina.

She sifted through it, then drew out an envelope, turning it over, and examining its foreign postmark before holding it out to Sara. "Another thick missive from Clayborn Montrose for you, Sara. From Paris, this time." She raised her eyebrows slightly. "He has become a frequent correspondent."

Sara took the letter without a word and put it down, unopened, beside her plate.

Annoyed, Georgina could not resist asking, "Aren't you going to read it?"

Sara continued buttering her toast. "Later," she replied coolly. She was nineteen now. Georgina could no longer expect to censor her mail.

Georgina tightened her lips in a gesture of disapproval but, determined not to rise to her stepdaughter's obvious bait, she checked any further comment and turned to her own sheaf of notes and invitations.

Satisfied that she had sufficiently displayed her indifference as well as her independence, Sara finished her breakfast. Then, pocketing Clay's letter, she excused herself and sauntered from the room.

Running upstairs to the privacy of her bedroom, she curled up on the window seat and eagerly ripped open the envelope.

After Katherine Maitland's wedding, when she had found out about Theo's engagement, the summer had dragged by, endless and bereft of joy for Sara. The only distraction from her lingering heartbreak were Clay's letters that came with surprising regularity.

Clay wrote with an easy fluidity, having a rare gift for describing the places he visited, so that they came to life under his pen. There was an openness, a naturalness about the letters that evoked Sara's pleasant impressions of the tall Virginian.

Though Clay had not been aware of it at the time, nor had Sara revealed it in her letters to him, she was grateful to him for saving her from utterly giving way to her emotions at Katherine Maitland's wedding reception. His flattering attentiveness had kept her in control all that long evening.

After Lucie had left for her final year at the Academe in Charleston, Sara was lonely, and his letters were a welcome diversion.

The image of him lingered. His soft drawl, his eyes full of warmth and laughter and something more, kindness.

His travels sounded exotic and exciting to Sara, who had traveled little and who longed for the experience of visiting other lands, tasting other cultures. To her, he was the ultimate cosmopolitan. His letters always ended with his desire to visit her in Savannah when he returned from Europe.

Sara sighed as she finished reading his letter. How she wished she could go abroad — or anywhere, just so she could escape her stepmother's petulant inquiries about her lack of interest in social life, the invitations that piled up, unanswered, on her dressing table. At first, Georgina had thought she must be sick, and had ordered Mammy to administer a tonic. But when Sara's ennui persisted, Georgina had become frantic.

Sara had tried to ignore her, riding out each morning for longer and longer periods of time, loath to return to the house to Georgina's nagging insistence that she accompany her to this or that social event. Most of all she yearned to escape from the lingering heartache of Theo's betrayal.

She spent hours alone, playing with Ruffy, and even took to reading some of the Jane Austen novels Lucie was so fond of, but a great deal of time was spent grieving for what might have been. She had retreated only to try to recover.

And Clay Montrose's letters had helped revive her. She would answer this one right away. In it he had hinted that there was something of great importance he wanted to ask her. Sara's curiosity was aroused.

Fall gave way to winter and Lucie came home for the Christmas holidays. Sara rallied enough to enter into the "coming out" party the Leightons hosted for their youngest daughter. Lucie had grown into a lovely young woman with her own delicate beauty, not Sara's spectacular good looks that stunned and sometimes intimidated, but a warm, winning radiance that brought her dozens of enchanted beaux.

Sara was happy for her sister but felt a curious detachment of interest in the young men who still clustered about *her* at parties. She felt as if she were waiting for something . . . or someone. What, or whom, she wasn't quite sure. Gradually, she came to realize that her future still held possibility and promise. The unknown had always appealed to Sara's adventurous spirit. As her bruised heart began to heal, she began to ask herself what might happen when Clay Montrose returned to Savannah.

Sometimes Sara even wondered if Clayborn Montrose was really that knight on a white charger that Lucie had always proclaimed would someday rescue her sister and carry her off to a beautiful castle far away.

The day she received word that Clay was on his way to Savannah, she was filled with unexpected excitement. He would be staying again with the Faxton Pierce family, he wrote, and would send a request to call as soon as he arrived.

His note and a bouquet were delivered when the family was at breakfast. After reading it, Georgina looked up with an expression of surprise and satisfaction.

"I have just received a gracious note from Clayborn Montrose, Sara, asking if he might call on you this afternoon."

Sara felt her heart give a little leap of pleasure, but she affected stifling a yawn, tossed back her hair with a little shrug, and poured more tea into her porcelain cup.

"He has just returned from his European travels, he says, so it should be an interesting visit," Georgina went on, curbing her impatience with Sara's lack of response. How annoying the girl was! Piqued, Georgina could not resist making a point. "Fortunately, it is my 'at home' day. Otherwise, I should have to ask him to come another day as my calendar is filled for the rest of the week."

Georgina had been favorably impressed with Clayborn Montrose when she had met him at Katherine's wedding. Moreover, she had made it her business to check up on him, and she had found no flaws. His background was impeccable. Heir to one of the largest James River plantations and fortunes, she had dubbed this a prestigious match for her stepdaughter. If only Sara — Georgina glanced again at Sara, realizing with fresh resolve just how much she wanted this girl safely married and in her own home, a long way from Savannah!

Sara rose leisurely, folded her napkin, and replaced it carefully into the silver ring engraved with her name, and asked to be excused.

"Well, I hope you're aware of the significance of this call, Sara," Georgina said sharply. "It's not every day you entertain the heir to a fortune."

Sara shrugged. "It's been nearly a year since I met him. I don't really remember him all that well, after all," she replied, unwilling to give Georgina the satisfaction of seeing her own interest in the purpose of Clay's call. "We'll just have to see."

Georgina decided she could play the game as well as Sara and refrained from further comment, merely calling after her stepdaughter's departing figure, "I suggest you wear your new flowered muslin afternoon dress, Sara."

Clay was shown into the Leightons' drawing room, where he was received cordially by Georgina, who was entertaining some ladies for tea.

After they had visited for the requisite quarter hour, conversing politely about the weather, his journey, his impressions of Europe, Georgina said, "Sara is in the garden, Mr. Montrose. I'm sure she will be delighted to see you again. You may go out that way." She indicated the louvered doors through which the brick walled garden was plainly visible, subtly suggesting that, while Clay had permission to be with Sara alone, their encounter could be viewed from the drawing room, and thus properly chaperoned.

Unsure of her own feelings, Sara was experiencing some ambivalence about Clay's visit. Something told her it held the key that might open the door of freedom to her. She did not know how much longer she could endure living under the same roof with the insufferable Georgina. On the other hand, was Clay, practically a stranger, the answer?

Even Mammy June noticed her nervousness as she dressed for his expected arrival. Two or three dresses were brought out to be tried on, then discarded, before Sara reluctantly settled for the new flower-strewn muslin Georgina had suggested. She swirled her hair up, let it fall around her shoulders, then tied it back with a wide blue satin ribbon.

Finally she threw down her brush, whistled for Ruffy, and ran down the back stairs and out into the garden without making the required appearance in the drawing room to greet Georgina's callers.

Sara needed this time before seeing Clay. For some reason her heart was pounding and her thoughts flying every which way.

It annoyed her, too, that Georgina was so anxious to make this visit important. Her stepmother had made no secret of the fact that she hoped Clay would propose, but Sara didn't even know if she wanted to get married. To put an end forever to the carefree life she had enjoyed as a belle? To go to Virginia to live? Virginia was so far away! It would mean leaving Lucie, her father, Savannah — everything familiar! No, she wasn't at all sure this was what she wanted.

While she waited, she amused herself by tossing a ball for Ruffy to fetch. When the spaniel tired of the game and flopped, panting, under the shade of the giant oak tree, Sara sat down on the swing. Her hair ribbon had come loose, and her heavy, dark hair was hot on her neck. She lifted it with both hands.

Pushing the swing idly with one foot, she let her mind wander. It traveled a well-worn path to thoughts of Theo Richardson. Would she ever get over that hurt? She had tried. But there were many nights when she still cried herself to sleep.

It was wrong, she knew. Theo was married now. She should not think of him anymore, she told herself. Still, she couldn't help wondering if he were happy. Did he ever think of her, regret what he had done?

To stop the ache, she tried to shut out the picture of him she carried in her mind — the thick-lashed eyes so amazingly blue in his dark-skinned face, the mouth with its slightly melancholy smile, the sensuous curve of the lips that had kissed hers so tenderly, but the dart of pain his memory brought was so piercing that Sara unconsciously drew in her breath.

To distract herself, she leaned forward to check on the kittens nestled close to her tabby in a basket under the tree. She bent down and scooped up the white one, cuddling him. She was holding it up to her cheek, nuzzling its furry head with her chin, when Clay stepped out onto the terrace. She looked up and smiled.

His first thought when he saw them was that both pairs of eyes were of the same startling hue. His second, how unbelievably lovely Sara was! He felt his heart contract in longing and love.

He moved toward her eagerly.

Never in all the years that followed could Clay quite recreate the hour they spent together in the blossoming fragrance of that Savannah garden. He knew that all his well-rehearsed speeches were soon forgotten as he basked in the presence of the object of his love.

What they spoke about, what they discussed, all remained dim in his mind. He only knew that he shared his feelings openly and that Sara had listened without stopping him, without rejecting his offer of a lifelong love.

He had not meant to speak so soon of marriage or of the future he desired they spend together. But when he left the garden that day, he knew Sara was considering his proposal, for she gave him permission to speak to her father.

If he remembered little else, Clay would never forget their first kiss, its sweetness reminding him of the taste and heady sensation of wine from the famous scuppernong grapes at Montclair.

He had walked from the shadowy umbrella of the oak tree, where they had sat together, into the sunshine like a sleepwalker, dazed and without direction. Then, quite impetuously, he had danced a little jig. He was mad with love for Sara Leighton, grateful, tender, passionate in his desire to spend the rest of his life making her happy.

Clayborn had no idea what an impossible task this would prove to be.

Savannah
Fall 1831

The whirlwind courtship stunned Savannah society, and although pleased by the alliance with the prominent Montrose family of Virginia, Georgina went into a flurry of frenzied preparations for a December wedding.

Lucie, ever the romantic, was torn between being thrilled at the prospect of being maid of honor at the wedding and devastated at the thought of her sister's moving so far away.

"But you can come to visit and stay for as long as you want, Lucie!" Sara reassured her, and that seemed to satisfy her, temporarily at least.

The weeks before the wedding were hectic ones, filled with dressmaking appointments, fittings, selecting china patterns, and coordinating guest lists with the invitations to be engraved and sent out. Sara felt as if there could not possibly be enough hours in the days that came and went with quicksilver swiftness. She moved through these events detached somehow but with her usual outward assurance and poise. And then, somewhat suddenly it seemed, the week of the wedding itself was upon her.

A few days before the wedding, Georgina paid an unexpected visit to Sara's bedroom.

"There are some things I must discuss with you, Sara," she began without preamble. *"Alone."* She waited, pointedly, for Mammy June to take her leave, then followed to close the door securely behind the old woman, after peering into the hallway to be sure she was not loitering outside and able to overhear their conversation.

Sara fervently hoped that she was not in for a lecture on the duties and obligations of married life, since her stepmother was the last person on earth she would want to deliver such pronouncements. But it was something quite different that Georgina had come to say.

"Your father and I have decided you are to take Lizzie and your groom, Wilson, with you to Montclair. We will send Anson and Molly later, along with your trunks."

Sara was baffled. She knew Mrs. Montrose had at least twenty house servants, and she assumed Clay's stable was staffed with capable grooms and trainers. She also knew that Georgina, a stern mistress, prided herself on her orderly household of well-trained servants. In fact, Sara recalled, her stepmother had brought along her personal maid, Camella, two housemaids, Fronsy and Molly, and her own coachman, Anson, when she married Leonard Leighton and moved to Savannah to live. Sara was astonished that the usually self-centered woman was willing to part with two of them now.

"But why should I take *your* servants?" she asked.

"Because, Sara, you must surround yourself with people you can trust," Georgina replied with an enigmatic expression on her face.

"Does that mean you don't think the Montrose servants are trustworthy?"

Georgina looked annoyed. "I don't mean that at all, Sara. Why must you always twist the meaning of my words?" Her voice was taut with tension. "I never said anything to you or Lucie before, because I did not think it wise to frighten either of you, as young as you were then. And, of course, the Leighton servants were second generation to those belonging to your father's family. However —" Here she lowered her voice confidentially — "As you know, I was brought up by my grandmother, who instilled in me the need to be careful when managing one's . . . people. You see, she never forgot a childhood experience, a slave uprising less than thirty years ago." She paused, and Sara sat forward, listening intently. "A close friend of her own mother, known to be a kind, indulgent mistress, was murdered by her own slaves!" Georgina paused dramatically, allowing Sara to receive the full impact of her words.

"She was murdered in her bed, while she slept!" she went on. "A full-scale insurrection was avoided in this country, but it was thought to have been inspired by word of the events in San Domingo where a bloody rebellion occurred. White folk and their loyal black slaves escaped for their lives, bringing with them tales of unspeakable horrors!" Georgina shuddered. "It made an indelible impression on my grandmother, I can assure you, and she was ever after afraid of even her own servants. She warned us to train our people with a firm hand, expect obedience, and reward diligence and loyalty, but never to pamper, and always to be wary."

Sara shivered, her vivid imagination filling in the untold details of this story.

Georgina continued. "Now Lizzie is still in training as a lady's maid, so you'll have to be patient. But she is eager and teachable, so I think she will work out nicely. And you must be explicit as to how you want things done and insist on her doing them correctly. Understand?"

Sara nodded. She was still not sure why Georgina had felt it necessary to warn her in this way, a favor that did not seem consistent with their volatile relationship. But she thanked her stepmother and soon forgot the strange incident.

Finally all the trunks were packed, and all that remained in Sara's armoire were her satin wedding gown, the color of a seashell that might be found on a Georgia beach, and her handsome traveling outfit for the honeymoon trip to New Orleans aboard the *River Queen.*

At last the moment came when, on her father's arm, Sara descended the stairway of her childhood home to begin a new life with the clear-eyed young man who waited for her at the church.

Through the drift of her tulle veil, she saw his worshipful gaze as he turned, holding out his hand to lead her to the steps of the altar. Such adoration was daunting, but Sara accepted it as a challenge.

Although she was conscious of the part of her heart that would never belong to Clay

Montrose, she realized she had never done anything as important as taking the vows uniting them as husband and wife. "From this day forward" she intended to keep the promises she was making "to love, honor, and cherish" him, no mater what.

Montclair

Winter 1832

In the master suite at Montclair, seated at her small desk, the only piece of furniture she had brought from her Savannah bedroom, Sara sat down to write a letter to Lucie.

> You must plan to visit us soon! I miss you so much and long to see you, even though my life here is unbelievably perfect. We will have such fun together and you will be astounded at my performance in my new role as mistress of this great plantation house. It is far bigger and grander than I had imagined, Lucie. But everything runs smoothly, with my hardly having to lift a finger to command! You may tell Stepmama that Lizzie's training is coming along, and that Molly and Anson are fitting in well with the

Montrose servants, so there is nothing for her to worry about.

As for me, I reign here as queen, which is quite a contrast to my position in the Leighton household, as you well know.

I fell in love with Montclair the minute we rode through the gates. We arrived here, directly from our New Orleans honeymoon, during a beautiful snowfall. The grounds, evergreen trees and the roof of this rambling brick and clapboard house were all blanketed in white. It seemed an auspicious beginning to our new life — everything so spotless and untouched and just waiting for us — like the pages of the new journal Clay received from his Aunt Avril at Christmas.

Inside, everything was in readiness to welcome us. Fires burning in every fireplace, candles glowing, a hot punch and delicious meal to greet the weary travelers. We had spent a week in Williamsburg before coming here, being royally entertained by Clay's Barnwell kin and their many friends.

Clay's Aunt Avril, of course, was responsible for our warm reception here, and she informed us that while we were on our wedding trip she had decided to move into a charming little house on the estate, called Eden Cottage. She made a delightful little ceremony of handing over the house keys to me, saying, "Now *you* are in charge."

I like Avril, I think. Clay is absolutely devoted to her, of course, but I don't feel she wants to intrude in our lives. That will be a welcome change!

Avril has a handsome "gentleman admirer" who is a frequent caller and dined with us the first evening we were "home." He is a distinguished lawyer with an international practice — an uncle of Douglas Cameron, Katherine Maitland's husband. I haven't had a chance to visit Kate yet at their family home, Cameron Hall, but hope to remedy that soon.

I wonder if Avril would ever consider marrying again. Clay tells me her marriage was a storybook romance, and she may not want to think of replacing her first true love. But she is still a young woman and most attractive. Her hair is still glorious, a deep auburn, and she has a flawless complexion, and eyes as guileless as a child's. I feel I will become quite fond of her as I get to know her better.

I think (scratched out) I intend (scratched out) — I *will* be happy here.

Everything has been done for my happiness, so I would be wretchedly ungrateful if I were not happy.

Clay is a kind and wonderful husband, and I shall do my best to be a good wife to him. Only you, dear sister, know there was another I had hoped to marry. But I have tried to put all that behind me and look forward to the future here in Virginia. I have moved into a new life and I plan to live it, enjoy it, and make the most of it. And I am now married to a man who loves me to distraction. Surely I am a most fortunate woman.

Please come soon, Lucie. Clay tells me Mayfield is especially lovely in the spring and, equally appealing, there is an abundant supply of very eligible bachelors among the society here.

Or is there a special someone keeping you in Savannah? If so, then you really must come so I can give you all my newfound "matronly" advice before you do anything rash, like become engaged. So please write back right away and tell me you *are* coming. Better still, tell me *when* you will arrive and we'll meet you in Williamsburg!

Ever your loving sister,
Sara Leighton Montrose

Sara blotted her signature, then folded the pages. She took her stamp from one of the pigeonholes in the desk, lighted the taper to melt the wax, letting it drip onto the letter, then pressed the Montrose crest into the molten wax.

For a moment her hand hovered in front of a small door in the center of the desk. Then she withdrew it and rose, walking quickly to the hall to place her letter to her sister on the silver tray to be taken down to the river, where the mail packet boat would come the next morning.

The inlaid desk was not the only thing Sara had brought with her from Savannah. Inside its secret compartment were all the letters Theo had written her, which she could not bear to destroy. Not always, but *this* time, did Sara successfully resist the temptation to reread them.

To Sara's delight, within weeks, Lucie wrote that she had their father's permission to come to Virginia in the spring.

The prospect of Lucie's imminent visit filled Sara with joyful anticipation. Her spirits soared, diminishing the loneliness and strange depression that often plagued her at Montclair, despite the cheerful tone of her letter.

It was an elusive feeling Sara could not explain. There was no reason for it she could identify, for every whim was fulfilled by her adoring husband. It seemed to be Clay's greatest desire to indulge her every wish and to try to anticipate anything that might bring her pleasure.

The first few months after their return, the two did everything together. Clay made no secret of the fact that he enjoyed Sara's company above all others, and preferred having her with him to any other diversion. They rode horseback daily, ate at any hour Sara felt hungry. Frequently, they sent into Williamsburg where Sara could shop to her heart's content, see a play, or attend a party. She was so vivacious, so appreciative of all she was seeing and hearing that it never occurred to Clay that his wife was not as happy as she pretended to be.

Nor would Clay have dreamed that beneath the surface, Sara was vaguely aware of a deep yearning for something more than the perfection of the life she was leading. With the word that Lucie was really coming, Sara dismissed her occasional melancholy as a passing mood.

The sisters had so much to say to each other, so much news to exchange, that they spent the first hours talking. Inevitably, on the third day of Lucie's visit, the subject about which Sara could no longer contain her curiosity, came up.

"Tell me, Lucie," Sara began idly, "do you ever hear anything about Theo Richardson?"

Lucie looked uncomfortable.

"Come now, Lucie! I can see you *do* know something. What is it?"

"Why do you want to hear about *him* now, Sara? He's part of the past. You have all this now —" She made a sweeping gesture with her hands — "a beautiful home, a handsome husband who plainly adores you — why hear something that will only make you miserable?"

"Why should it make me miserable?" Sara demanded. Lucie's reticence was making her even more curious. "I just want to hear what you know. It has nothing to do with Clay or Montclair or me."

Lucie sighed. "Oh, all right, Sara. But it may all be gossip, remember."

"For heaven's sake, Lucie. Do go on!"

"Well, he and Evangeline come to Savannah often now. Theo is working for the Archer Shipbuilding Company as a designer, and he consults with some of the Savannah builders, I suppose. Anyway, they stay with friends of her family." Lucie halted as if trying to decide whether to continue.

"And? What else, Lucie?" Sara urged.

"Nothing really. I mean, it's just an impression —"

"What kind of impression? Lucie, you're maddening!"

"I've only seen them once, at a party at the Pierces' and —" She paused, then rushed on. "He looked . . . well . . . sad. He has such tragic eyes," she finished dramatically.

Sara's heart wrenched. She remembered those eyes. They had not seemed tragic then. They had had a soft radiance, gentle and thoughtful, shining with love as they gazed into her own. Her throat tightened painfully.

"Is that all? What about Evangeline? Does she also look *tragic?*" There was a twist of irony in the question.

"No, not exactly. More . . . pensive, I'd say. Actually, the two of them weren't even together that night. She can't dance, of course, so she was sitting on the side, visiting with some of the older ladies."

"And Theo? What of Theo?"

Lucie sighed again. "I'm sorry to say he frequented the punch bowl the entire evening."

"He didn't get . . . no! You don't mean —" Sara gasped.

"Oh, no. Theo is ever the gentleman. It's just that he didn't dance, he didn't socialize, and he didn't even attend his wife." Lucie's voice faded away.

Sara gave Lucie a hard look. She knew her sister. Lucie wasn't telling everything. "And what else, Lucie? There's something more, isn't there?"

"All right, Sara, if you must know. This spring the Archer Company launched a new ship with great fanfare. The mayor, members of the city council, all sorts of prominent Charlestonians were present. There was to be a huge reception afterwards —"

"But what has that to do with — ?"

"Wait, Sara, I'm coming to that. It was a beautiful ship with a figurehead that Theo himself had designed and carved. Mr. Archer had planned for Evangeline to christen the ship. And, as it was unveiled . . . well —" Lucie seemed unable to continue.

"For pity's sake, don't keep me panting with suspense, Lucie. What happened?"

"Nothing *happened,* Sara. It was just that the face on the figurehead . . . that is, it looked familiar . . . at least, everyone who was there who knows you, *said* —"

"Said *what?*" Sara felt as if her heart

would stop beating.

"Said it looked like *you,* Sara!"

Sara stared, speechless, at her sister.

"Worse still, they named the ship *The Savannah Belle.*" Lucie watched Sara carefully before rushing on. "Of course, the Archers have no idea unless some gossip decides to enlighten them. Poor Evangeline! But then she wasn't at the Academe when you were there, so she would not know that the figurehead bears a resemblance to any living person. To tell the truth, I suspect even Theo doesn't realize what he's done. I think he simply carved the figure from memory, your image so printed in his mind that he just drew it unconsciously."

Sara felt herself grow faint. Although her face revealed nothing, her heart spoke volumes. Theo had no more forgotten her than she had forgotten him! Each was indelibly etched in the other's being.

"Oh, Sara, I didn't want to tell you, but you insisted!" Lucie was pleading now. "I had so hoped you and Theo could forget each other and be happy with your new lives. Sara, you certainly have everything you need to make you happy here."

"I know, Lucie. And if Theo is unhappy, he has only himself to blame. He had the soul of an artist and he sold it for security." Sara felt her heart harden, grow cold within her.

"Don't be sad, Sara. Oh, I wish you hadn't made me tell you!" Lucie moaned.

"It's all right, Lucie. I would possibly have heard it anyway from someone. Katherine Cameron has visitors from Charleston. They've probably brought the latest gossip with them."

Outwardly calm, Sara quickly changed the subject. For the remainder of Lucie's visit they did not speak of Theo Richardson again.

Sara was desolate when her sister left. Since neither was certain how long it would be before they saw each other, their parting was tearful. Both knew, but did not verbalize, the fact that Sara did not feel welcome to come to Savannah without a specific invitation from their stepmother.

Clay escorted Lucie to Williamsburg, putting her on the stage to Norfolk to return to Savannah by ship. As soon as the carriage had disappeared around the bend of the drive, Sara had her horse saddled and rode deep into the woods.

She galloped past Eden Cottage, empty since Avril was visiting friends in North Carolina, and up the ridge to the plateau overlooking the river. There she dismounted, tethered Cheval to a nearby tree, and walked to the edge, gazing down at the silvery ribbon of water glistening below.

Sara was bereft. Although Lucie had enjoyed her visit, Sara knew her sister was anxious to return to Savannah and to the young man with whom she was now in love. Loneliness enveloped Sara in an immense cloud of sadness, and she began to sob. Her tears were not only for the loss of a beloved sister, but for all the other losses of her life. Most of her tears, however, were for the love she had never truly relinquished.

"Wrong! Wrong! I know it's wrong to feel this way," she cried brokenly. Guilt and the conviction of disloyalty to Clay only intensified her grief.

Gradually her sobs lessened. Sara wiped her eyes with the sleeve of her jacket and turned to remount her horse. She stood at his head, rubbing the velvety nose, patting the arched neck. Worn out from emotion, she leaned against him for consolation.

The woods were silent except for the sound of birdsong high in the branches above her, and below, rushing water over rocks in the river.

What was one person's sadness in the whole scheme of things? What did it matter that her own heart was broken when everything about her went on as before, with no thought of *her* pain?

Was it true that " 'Tis better to have loved and lost than never to have loved at all"? Were poets really wiser than ordinary folk, or only facile with words? Did heartbreak serve any purpose?

It must have some value, Sara thought desperately. Why else would one suffer so much if not for some reason? Into her mind, unbidden, came another quotation: "Everything works together for good to those who love the Lord and are called to His purpose."

Where had she heard those words? And why was she remembering them now? Whatever had been the reason for loving Theo and losing him, she knew she must make herself put him out of her mind. Leave it behind forever. She must try to love Clay as he deserved to be loved. She was determined to do that.

People always said she was stubborn. But Sara had denied it, saying instead, "Not stubborn. Strong."

Well, now she would prove it. Whatever it took, she would get over this destructive obsession with Theo, what might have been.

Determinedly, Sara remounted, turned Cheval around, and rode out of the shadowy woods into the sunlight and on toward Montclair.

Montclair
1835

chapter 10

Frost etched the windowpanes in the master suite at Montclair. Outside, the snow that had fallen a few days before remained in frozen patches on the winter brown grass. Although it was not yet evening, the day had darkened early and it had been necessary to light candles throughout the house.

Sara sat at her dressing table, having Lizzie dress her hair in preparation for the traditional New Year's Day open house at Cameron Hall.

"No, Lizzie, don't brush it so high. Here, I'll show you what I mean." She took the brush out of the girl's hand. "I like some curls around my face. It's softer that way, not so severe."

Lizzie, a slip of a girl with light brown skin and observant eyes, watched her mistress deftly bring a few tendrils of dark hair fetchingly over her temples and ears.

"See? That's the effect I want," Sara explained, handing Lizzie the brush. She knew she must curb her natural impatience with the young maid, try to remember she was still young and inexperienced. But Lizzie was also bright and clever with her hands, and Sara was more than pleased with her progress.

Quickly Lizzie made the finishing touches on the elaborate coiffure, carefully inserting a high-backed marcasite-studded comb, then stepped back to survey her handiwork.

Pleased with herself, Lizzie smiled. "You look mahty fine, Miss Sara."

"The word is *beautiful,*" came Clay's enthusiastic comment as he entered from his dressing room.

"But then, you're so terribly prejudiced! You are ever the gallant gentleman, Clay Montrose, so I never know whether to believe your compliments or not!" Sara said mockingly as he strode into the room and crossed to cup her shoulders in his hands. "It's not you I'm trying to impress, if you must know. I must look grand for all the ladies of Mayfield County who will be at Katherine and Doug's party. And I dare say they are much more critical than you!"

"No one will hold a candle to you, my darling," Clay replied, leaning down to place his cheek against hers. His gaze, reflected in her gilt-framed mirror, was tender.

"Is it time to go?" Sara asked, shifting slightly to look up at him.

"Not quite. I have something I want you to wear tonight."

"What do you mean? I selected this gown with your preference for blue in mind."

"You're devastating in blue, dearest. No, this is something that will only furnish the icing on the cake." And, from the pocket of his swallow-tailed coat, Clay brought out a velvet jewel case and pressed the spring. Sara's eyes widened in amazement at the jewels inside. A king's ransom, she thought, reaching over to touch the exquisite necklace and matching pendant earrings. The rubies flamed with dazzling blazes of fire — the diamonds were circlets of tiny glittering stars.

"Clay, they're magnificent!" breathed Sara.

"Aren't they? I didn't even know about them until the letter from Aunt Avril. She had forgotten all about them. That's not surprising, knowing how unworldly she is." He smiled affectionately at this insight. "She herself never wore the jewels, so they have been in the wall safe in the plantation office all this time. Now she — and I, of course — want you to wear the Montrose bridal set. Here, let me put the necklace on for you."

He fastened it around Sara's slender neck. The clasp felt heavy and cold against her skin. Regarding her image in the glass, Sara tentatively fingered the dazzling jewels.

"I have never seen anything so beautiful!" she said, and her hands shook a little as she slipped the matching earrings into the lobes of her ears.

"They were made for you, Sara!" Clay declared triumphantly. "You look like a queen."

Lizzie stepped from the shadows to bring Sara her midnight-blue velvet evening cape, and handed it to Clay, who placed it gently around Sara's shoulders. Sara took the small ermine muff and white kid gloves Lizzie handed her. Then, with a final glance in the mirror, said, "Now I'm ready."

As Sara, on his proud arm, swept into the drawing room at Cameron Hall, other eyes confirmed Clay's quiet conviction. There was no question that the new Mrs. Montrose was stunning.

In spite of the bad weather that had

plagued the area since Christmas, Cameron Hall was filled with guests come together to celebrate the New Year. Many who had traveled a great distance from the widely spaced plantation homes along the James River, were houseguests.

Virginians were as well known for their partying at every opportunity as Cameron Hall was famous for its hospitality. It would never have occurred to either the guests or their host to allow the weather to delay a tradition they had looked forward to all year.

The house was still festively decorated for Christmas, with garlands of fragrant greens festooning walls and windows. Bright red bayberry candles shone from the sparkling crystal chandeliers, enhancing the glorious colors of the ladies' gowns as they spun with their partners in the old country dances. It was a happy mingling of good conversation, music, dancing, and merriment combined with fine wine and well prepared food.

Watching Katherine move graciously among her guests, Sara could not prevent a small twinge of envy at her friend's ease and evident popularity. Just as Katherine Maitland had been one of the most popular girls in school, Mrs. Douglas Cameron had won an assured position in the close-knit Mayfield society, even though she was as much an "outsider" as Sara.

Sara had never felt the need for close girlfriends. Lucie had always been her best friend. But now, far from Savannah and sister, Sara fervently wished that she and Katherine might become close.

Katherine possessed other qualities that Sara admired and secretly envied. For all her radiant beauty, Katherine was genuinely kind, generous, outgoing. At school everyone had wanted to be Katherine Maitland's friend.

Doug Cameron obviously doted on his wife. During the long evening, he seemed never to be more than a step away from her. Though Sara knew Clay loved her just as ardently, he was more reserved in public, keeping his expressions of affection for their private moments. Still, for some reason, seeing the Camerons so in love and not afraid to show it, annoyed Sara.

At last the evening drew to an end, and at Katherine's bidding, a circle was formed and the guests joined hands to sing "Auld Lang Syne" in the time-honored Scottish tradition. At the conclusion, Sara went to retrieve her wrap, and Katherine followed her into the downstairs bedroom used as a ladies' "retiring room."

Alone in there, Katherine gave Sara an

impulsive hug. "Sara, I have the most marvelous news! I cannot keep it to myself a minute longer! I have to tell someone. Sara, I'm going to have a child!"

Later, on the way back to Montclair in their horse-drawn sleigh, Sara was quiet. Even with Clay's arm holding her close under the fur-lined robe, she felt cold and withdrawn. The gaiety and excitement of the evening had flown and she was strangely melancholy. Why on earth should she feel this way, she asked herself when, in Lucie's words, she had "everything" to make her happy?

They had been sitting under the trees on the velvety lawn when Lucie made a startling observation. "Well, Sara, who would ever have imagined that all your dreams would come true?"

She gave a wry laugh. "What dreams?"

Her sister seemed puzzled. "Surely, you aren't still thinking of Theo, after all I told you?"

"But all that might not have happened if he and I —"

"Oh, Sara, I hope you aren't ever so foolish as to wish that things had turned out differently! If Theo were half the man Clayborn Montrose is —"

These troubling thoughts came to a halt as

the carriage drew up in front of Montclair.

A fire was glowing in their bedroom fireplace, and Lizzie, who had waited up for her mistress, brought in a tray with a pot of hot chocolate and some fruitcake. She took Sara's cape, offered her a warm mohair shawl, and drew her chair closer to the warmth of the fire.

"Is there anything else you'd like me to do, Miss Sara?" she asked softly.

"No, go to bed, Lizzie. I won't need you anymore tonight," Sara told her and the little maid left.

Clay removed his jacket and flung it over the other wing chair opposite Sara's before pouring them both a cup of hot chocolate.

"Did you enjoy yourself tonight?" he asked, handing her a cup.

Sara took a sip before replying. She studied her husband, wondering if she should express herself honestly. Actually, she had been thinking how much she would like to give a party at Montclair, a brilliant one that might rival the Camerons'. But that did not seem quite appropriate. Instead, she smiled and suggested, "It's made me want to do some entertaining here. This is such a lovely house, and we have already acquired several social obligations we ought to return."

"Splendid idea!" Clay seemed enthusiastic. "Aunt Avril wasn't much for party-giving, and Uncle Graham was rather reclusive. Besides, they seemed to have no need for other people in their lives, seemed to find each other sufficient." He paused in reflection, then laughed. "Of course, we always had a houseful of Aunt Avril's itinerant preachers! They'd start coming in the spring and kept on coming right on through the fall. Feeding the overflow from tent meetings and revivals was about the extent of their entertaining."

Clay, glancing over at Sara, thought *How lovely she looks in the firelight.* "I'm so glad you like the Camerons as much as I do, darling. Doug's been my best friend since boyhood. And, of course, you and Katherine were schoolmates. What a wonderful couple they are!"

Sara felt a prickle of irritation. She feigned a yawn before saying languidly, "Well, I do become a little weary of Doug's constant fawning over Katherine."

Clay frowned. "I don't know what you mean."

"Don't you find Doug a bit uxorious? Every time he spoke to Katherine or about her, it was 'my sweet Kate' this, or 'Kate, darling' that!" Sara's mimicry was tinged with sarcasm.

Clay did not respond to her implied derision. Instead, he said thoughtfully, "Perhaps his tenderness shows the degree of intimacy they share."

Sara shrugged. "Perhaps," she conceded, wishing now she had not said anything and hoping against hope that Clay was not angry with her for her comment about his friends.

For a few minutes there was no sound in the room other than the crackle of the fire. She felt an unaccustomed uneasiness as Clay became silent, staring thoughtfully into the burning embers.

At last he broke the silence. "I think Doug and Katherine are as close as two people can be. They seem to have a relationship something like Aunt Avril and Uncle Graham had — kindred spirits so close they can almost read each other's thoughts, know what the other will say before he says a word." Clay leveled his clear gaze on Sara. "Whereas with *you*, my darling —" He hesitated before continuing — "I adore you, Sara, but I don't really know you. You are like that little desk you brought with you from Savannah — full of secret drawers, hidden places, and locked corners to which I have no key."

Icy fingers clutched Sara's heart. He had compared her to the desk where the deepest secret of her heart was locked! Theo's love letters! Could he have possibly guessed? No, of course not. Still, guilt was heavy upon her.

Clay's words hung there between them for a long moment, his eyes holding Sara's until she could not look away. Slowly, she got up from her chair and came over to him, kneeling before him on the floor.

"I don't want to be like that, Clay. I want you to know me — as I am, with nothing tucked away, held back, kept from you. I want you to love me, just as I am, with no illusions, with all the crevices and cracks and flaws. That's the only way I can feel safe. I love that little desk, not because it is valuable . . . it is veneered. But underneath, it is solid and sturdy and durable." She looked long into his eyes. "You see only the polished surface of me. I want you to love the woman beneath!"

Clay lifted Sara to her feet, took her in his arms and kissed her deeply. She heard him murmur her name against her lips. She held him, longing to be lost in strong, lasting love. This was the man she was committed to forever. With him she wanted to find the kind of happiness she had never known.

On the second day of 1835 a cold, icy rain

fell steadily, drumming a funereal beat on the roof and against the windows in sharp contrast to the spritely music Sara had danced to the night before.

Restlessly, she roamed the house, moving from room to room as if searching for something. In the small music room stood an old-fashioned harpsichord in exile from an earlier day and replaced by the large piano now in residence at one end of the drawing room. As she stood there, sliding her hand along the covered keyboard, she wondered who had played it before, how it had come to be at Montclair. Never much of a musician herself, despite the hours of lessons she had endured, Sara nevertheless admired its quaint shape, the hand-painted floral designs on the fine-grained wood, then noticed the framed sampler hanging above it.

The yarn with which it had been embroidered was faded. Still, it was readable, and the name stitched at the bottom was *NORAMARY MARSH MONTROSE A.D. 1745* — almost one hundred years ago! Noramary, the *first* bride of Montclair. A turreted house at the top was identified as "My Birthplace," MONKSMOOR PRIORY, Kent England; under that, a sailing ship named *FAIRWINDS*; next, a yellow cottage with picket fence, a row of flowers and then a Scripture verse, "Delight thyself in the Lord; and He will give thee the desires of thine heart — Psalm 37:4."

As Sara repeated the words aloud, she felt a pang of guilt. Since leaving school she had neglected Bible reading and daily devotionals. But the words of this verse were vaguely familiar and struck a responsive chord within her.

What were the real "desires of her heart"? And if she knew and asked the Lord for them, would he give them to her?

Sara wandered over to the window and stared out. The rain-soaked landscape was miserably dreary. Pressing her face against the panes, she was filled with an inexpressible longing. A longing for what?

For some reason Kate Cameron came to mind. She saw Katherine's radiant face when she had told Sara about the coming baby. She felt her heart contact. A baby, a son for Clay, a child to live in this house, make it a true home, inherit this beautiful place someday. Right then, Sara knew *that* was the real desire of her heart.

Almost miraculously she felt calmer, and a kind of peace seemed to envelop her. Why had she not thought of it before? Maybe that was the missing piece, that void in her that never seemed to be filled.

"Ask and ye shall receive." Was it really that simple? All one had to do was ask?

No, Sara thought. *Surely it isn't that easy. You have to be good for God to answer your prayers.* She was far from good. Sara felt her face grow hot as she recalled all the countless small, mean, selfish things she had done in her life. She would have to be better, try harder.

But *Clay* was good. Oh, yes, Clay was certainly "righteous" as the Bible said. And his Aunt Avril — surely her prayers were answered. She would write Avril and ask her to pray that she and Clay would have a child, a son!

Yes, she would do that right away. Today!

Part III

Montclair

Summer 1842

chapter 11

On the side lawn Sara was supervising six-year-old Malcolm and Bryson, a sturdy two-year-old, playing with the five new setter puppies when Kate Cameron came riding up in her landau, escorted by the redheaded twins on their ponies.

Kate waved her buggy whip and rounded the curve of the driveway before halting her high-stepping chestnut mare in the leafy shade of one of the giant elms.

"Did the boys ride the whole way?" Sara asked, getting to her feet and walking over to greet Katherine.

"Yes, indeed, they insisted, although I offered to spell them at the halfway point." Katherine laughed, looking with pride at her twins as they dismounted and looped their reins over the black iron hitching post in front of the house.

"And they're only five!" mused Sara, mentally deciding to increase Malcolm's practice hours in the riding ring. She was determined Rod and Stewart Cameron's equestrian skills would not surpass her son's, even though he was a full year older.

Sara was no longer so conscious of her deep-rooted, though subtle, rivalry with Katherine Cameron except when it came to the boys. She intended them to excel in everything. Secretly she knew she could not compete with Kate in most aspects — sterling character, her reputation as a hostess — unless it was, perhaps, on horseback. She only knew she wanted her sons to be the best riders in Mayfield County.

Katherine followed the twins as they ran over to inspect the puppies that were tumbling all over each other.

"What darlings!" Katherine said, bending over to touch one's soft furriness.

"The twins can choose one each to take home — if you'll allow it," offered Sara.

"Are you sure? That's very generous, Sara."

"Yes, they're almost weaned and in another week or so, they'll be quite ready to be on their own."

The two women settled themselves on the swing beneath the shade of the sweeping elm, watching affectionately the four little boys playing with the puppies — two curly-haired carrot tops, Malcolm's dark silky head and Bryson's cornsilk blond one, all bumping together along with the scrambling brown-white-and-gold wriggling bodies of the pups.

"What do you hear from Savannah, Sara?" Kate asked.

"Not much recently. Lucie is so busy with her new house. They're building on land given to them by Brockton's father for a wedding present."

"It's too bad you weren't able to attend her wedding, Sara."

"Well, yes, but I was expecting Bryson at the time, you may recall, and it was impossible for me to travel so far."

"Of course, nothing is worth risking losing a baby for," sighed Katherine. Both were silent for a moment, remembering the disappointment Kate had experienced when she had suffered a miscarriage with her first pregnancy.

So grieved were the Camerons over the loss of their expected child that Sara and Clay tried to minimize their own joy at Malcolm's birth for their friends' sake. But then eighteen months later, the twins were born and Kate and Doug were ecstatic. As if not to be outdone, the next year Sara had Bryson.

Sara and Katherine chatted about mutual Mayfield friends and upcoming social events while the children played.

"Why don't we go inside and have tea?" Sara suggested after several pleasant minutes. "I'll have Becca come out to mind the boys."

On the porch Ruffy, now old, fat, and arthritic, struggled to his feet from the place where he had been sleeping in the sun, and followed his mistress into the house. It was pleasantly cool inside, in contrast to the warm spring afternoon.

Sara led the way into the drawing room. She went over to the fireplace and tugged the embroidered bell pull. Almost immediately a woman servant appeared.

"Yes'm, Miz Sara?" She bobbed a little curtsy.

"Lu, please bring us tea and some of the lemon poppyseed cake and tell Becca to go out to the children. She can take them some grape juice and cookies," Sara instructed. "And tell her to hurry." Casting a watchful eye out the window, she continued, "Bryce tries so hard to do everything Malcolm does. I can't leave them alone for a minute. They're busy with the puppies now, but if they should decide to get on the ponies —" Sara stood there until she saw Becca coming around the side of the house, then she turned back to Kate.

"Would you believe that Bryce cries when I put on my riding habit? I have to set him up on the saddle in front of me and ride around the circle a few times. Then, when I hand him back to Becca, he starts wailing again. I declare, he's going to be an Arab on horseback."

"And what about Malcolm?" asked Kate.

"Oh, he's fearless, a natural. Of course, I put him on his own pony when he was three. I'm beginning to teach him to jump," Sara said proudly.

"Like mother, like son," commented Kate. "I've never known anyone as brave on a horse as you, Sara."

"Clay would call it reckless, I'm afraid."

"But he doesn't seem to object," Kate remarked.

"Object? He wouldn't dare!" Sara spoke with mock indignation and yet there was a trace of seriousness underlying her words.

Kate shook her head. "I don't doubt that for a minute. After he agreed to let you drop the word *obey* from your marriage vows, Clay didn't stand a chance!"

Sara pretended shock. "How did you know that?"

"Oh, come, Sara, it was the talk of the town after your wedding!"

"Savannah has little enough to talk of

then!" she retorted haughtily, then gave an amused shrug. "Actually, I was just so nervous repeating the vows that I simply forgot to say all the words."

"Sara! You really expect me to believe *that?*" scoffed Kate.

"Believe what you like!" Sara's eyes sparkled mischievously.

"Don't forget, Sara, I was at school with you. I *know* about some of your pranks!"

"Ah, dear old Madame Couvoisier's!" Sara rolled her eyes. "How did we ever live through it all? Those dreary lessons, being made to sit straight against a backboard, and only allowed to speak French at meals! I nearly starved to death my first year until I learned at least to say *passez moi la panne* and *cafe au lait s'il vous plait!*"

"Well, at least we came out with good posture and a smattering of French." Kate smiled.

When the tea tray was brought in, cups poured, cake passed, Katherine launched another discussion. "Did I tell you I am going to take the boys to my parents for a visit in the fall?"

"You're going to Savannah?"

"Yes, in October."

Sara's hand holding her teacup began to tremble, and she set it down. She was suddenly seized with a rush of her old anger at her stepmother, a deep resentment that Katherine could so easily "go home" while she remained an exile from her father's house. Georgina had made it no secret she was glad to have Sara out of her life.

Unaware of her hostess's inner distress, Katherine went on. "Yes, Papa has not been too well lately, and Mama doesn't want to leave him, so my going there seems the best plan."

"How long will you be gone?" Sara asked through stiff lips.

"About a month. Douglas will join us later and bring us back before Christmas. Actually, it is going to be something of a family reunion. Some of mother's relatives are planning to visit at the same time."

Sara, who had picked up her teacup again, felt her fingers grip the delicate handle tightly. Would the "reunion" include the Maitlands' relatives from Charleston, the Richardsons? She wondered, but would not allow herself to ask.

"I'm going to the Springs in a few weeks myself," Sara told Kate, only that minute making up her mind to do so.

"Oh, aren't you well, Sara?" There was a questioning concern in Kate's glance.

"I'm fine. I just feel the urge to get away

for a while. The children are so demanding, don't you agree? It is so restorative there. I come back feeling full of life and energy."

"But you never seem to be any other way, Sara."

"Yes, but there they encourage women to be more active. I'm afraid we are much too pampered here. Look how long the doctors want to keep you in bed after having a baby! Six weeks! Why, I'd be as weak as a kitten if I stayed confined that long!"

"But, surely, the doctors know what is best —" Kate sounded doubtful.

"Dr. Erling? He's a nice old gentleman, Kate, but not at all advanced. I simply refused to follow his instructions after I had Bryce. I learned from having Malcolm that it wasn't necessary for me to be so inactive." Sara lowered her voice conspiratorially. "In fact, Kate, I read recently that hydropathists declare that a great deal of the pain of childbirth women endure can be prevented!"

"How?" asked Kate, leaning forward, evidently remembering the twins' birth.

"They advocate massage, and bathing in warm water to relax you in preparation. Then the actual delivery is assisted by nurses trained in hydropathy. Women who have undergone this method report they are up and walking about and feeling fine on the third day after the birth!"

"Really?"

"Indeed!" declared Sara. "Of course, they suggest you come to the clinic weeks before you are due and enter into a routine of walking, drinking mineral water, the baths, and a very healthful diet. Furthermore, if I have another child, I am determined to spend the last three months at such a clinic."

"And not have yours and Clayborn's child born at Montclair?"

"Malcolm will inherit Montclair, Kate, and *he* was born *here*. That's all that's necessary."

The boisterous sound of children's voices outside interrupted their conversation, and Katherine put down her teacup and got to her feet.

"I really must be going, Sara. The boys have a long ride ahead of them. And Douglas will send out a search party for us if we're late." She laughed softly as she pulled on her driving gloves. "Thank you for the tea and the lovely gift of the pups. Shall we send over for them? Or, better still, why don't you bring the children and the puppies and come to Cameron Hall for the day or stay the night?"

"What a treat!" exclaimed Sara as she accompanied her guest to the door.

The boys were engaging in a minor shouting match as to which puppy each of them would claim, and the two women found themselves acting as arbiters. Bryson got excited and began to cry at all the noise, and Becca lifted him up into her ample arms and carried him into the house.

Finally, the choice of puppies was resolved and Malcolm put them all back in their basket, while the Cameron twins went to mount up for the trip home.

Sara stood waving goodbye as Kate's landau and the two little boys on their ponies headed down the drive toward the gate. As they rounded the bend, she felt a little hand slip into hers and she looked down into Malcolm's upturned face.

Her heart melted within her, and a surging joy swelled in her breast. What a treasure this child was, Sara thought. She leaned down and drew him close, relishing the special scent of his skin, the warmth of his silken curls against her cheek.

From the hour he had been laid in her arms and she had seen the exquisite perfection of him, Sara had been lost. She had never expected to feel that way about a child. All the time she had carried him, the baby had almost been abstract, something she had wanted for Clayborn. She was proud and happy to be bringing a son into this beautiful mansion, fulfilling the need for an heir to the vast estate of Montclair, yet the baby itself had not been real to Sara. Not until she had seen him, that is, and held him.

From the beginning, Malcolm had been part of Sara in some kind of extraordinary way she could never explain. He was a gift, she felt, meant to make up for everything she had yearned for, been deprived of, all that she had missed in every other relationship.

She would sit and hold him for hours, wondering at his perfection, experiencing an almost spiritual uplifting. She had been reluctant for Carrie, who became his nurse, to take him away even to bathe and dress him.

When Bryson was born, although she was grateful that she had been delivered of such a fine, healthy child, Sara realized that there had not been a similar bonding. She had welcomed Becca's eager care of the baby, and six weeks after his birth she had gone away to the Springs without a thought.

Yes, Malcolm was different. He was Sara's heart.

She kissed him now and, holding his hand, said, "Come, let's go in, darling. Mama will read you a story before supper."

chapter 12

Montclair
Mayfield, Virginia
December 1842

Dearest Lucie,

How I would love to be spending this holiday season with you, beloved sister. Alas, however, the distance and circumstances prevent it! Perhaps, someday —

I am sending your Christmas presents early because we are planning to spend several days in Williamsburg. The children are old enough now to enjoy some of the exciting festivities always part of the celebration there. We will be staying at the Barnwell house belonging to Clay's great-great Aunt Laura. Avril is there now, readying it for the arrival of Kitty Barnwell Camden, a cousin, who has inherited it.

Kitty married an English lord and went to England to live, but is now widowed and returning to Virginia.

Since the house has been closed for some years since the old lady's death, there is a great deal to be done. Avril was given the responsibility in Laura Barnwell's will to go through all her personal possessions, papers, and belongings, so she took two of her servants with her and has been away nearly three weeks.

Malcolm and Bryce are clamoring to see Nana, though Avril is really not their grandmother. Still, she dotes on the boys and they adore her. Avril has a way with all children, black and white! Wherever she goes around here, a little cluster of them follow, my own included! Avril should have had a dozen of her own.

So, we are all looking forward to celebrating Christmas in a very special and uniquely Williamsburg style this year. I wish you an equally happy Yuletide season in your new home. I hope the New Year will bring us both great happiness. Ever your devoted sister,

Sara Leighton Montrose

Williamsburg, Barnwell House

December 1842

Avril made her way up the narrow steps to the attic. The door opened with a creak of protest, and she stepped into the small, slant-roofed room at the top of the Barnwell house. Pale winter sunlight streamed in through the dormer windows.

She stood there a minute, looking around. The accumulation of years filled every foot of space. Boxes were piled one on top of the other under the eaves. Discarded furniture and other household goods were scattered, helter-skelter. Where to begin? And then Avril spotted the humpbacked trunk toward the front. Of worn, brown leather, darkened with dirt and age, studded with tarnished brass nails, and banded with thick straps, it stood a little apart from the rest of the clutter.

On the top, in faded gilt letters, the name *LAURA BARNWELL* identified its original owner. Aunt Laura had probably packed it when it was shiny and new — in 1745, when she went off to Miss Dale's Female

Academy — then unpacked it when she came home two years later, and sent it up to the attic, never to leave Williamsburg or Virginia again.

Avril knew there was a mystery surrounding Aunt Laura, though she did not know the full story. She had heard of a love affair broken off by a misunderstanding and that Aunt Laura, beautiful and charming as she was, had never married. Perhaps some of those secrets would be revealed in the contents of the trunk when she opened it.

At this moment she felt the full responsibility of Aunt Laura's trust. She regretted having waited so long to fulfill Laura's request, but so much had happened in Avril's own life since the old lady's death that she had not been free to carry out her duties until now. It had taken the startling news of Kitty Barnwell's return from England to bring Avril in to Williamsburg.

Taking the key from the pocket of her apron, Avril inserted it in the rusty lock and turned it. It moved slowly, the metal grating against the keyhole. Avril heard the latch click. Then, with both hands, she lifted the lid.

A slight musty odor, mixed with the faint scent of dried potpourri, tickled Avril's nose and she sneezed. Kneeling in front of the trunk, she folded back the crinkled lavender tissue paper covering the shallow first shelf. On top of yellowed but exquisitely embroidered linens was a letter addressed to Avril in Aunt Laura's fine, spidery script.

With hands that trembled a little, Avril picked it up, broke the seal, and drew out the letter her aunt had written her.

> My dear Avril, You have always been such a joy and comfort since you came into our family, I know I can trust you with the contents of this trunk. Some of the things herein are not mine but have been passed on to me by others, so please be a faithful custodian of all it contains and act with great discretion in everything pertaining to them.
>
> I began keeping a journal as a child, at my dear mother's directive, as a kind of discipline. She always taught that this was a fine record of one's spiritual progress as well as a safe repository for thoughts and feelings. These journals were always kept private, and so I ask that you read them, if you like, with the understanding that some were written with the innocent spontaneity of children, and some with the impulsiveness of immaturity. All should be consid-

ered in the light of the times in which they were written and the age of the diarist.

There is also, herein, a packet of letters given to my mother, extracting from her the solemn promise that on the death of the correspondents, they would be destroyed. Since my mother, Elizabeth Barnwell, died before being able to carry out that promise, this was not done.

I feel I can confide in you that they were letters written between Noramary Marsh and Robert Stedd before she became Duncan Montrose's wife and the first bride of Montclair. They had been childhood sweethearts and planned to marry. But when my older sister Winnie, Duncan's fiancée, eloped with our French tutor practically on the eve of the wedding, Noramary agreed to save the family honor as well as safeguard the sizeable dowry that had already been paid, by becoming Winnie's substitute.

Noramary was heartbroken but in time, I believe, came to love Duncan dearly and they were very happy together. I don't know if she forgot she had given these letters to Mama, but she never asked for them back. Robert Stedd never married.

Robert Stedd! That name was familiar. Avril leaned back on her heels. Was that old Dr. Stedd? The image of an erect white-haired figure came to mind. She had seen the old physician many times, walking or driving his carriage along the Williamsburg streets. Why, the Stedd house was only a few houses down from the Barnwells! A handsome blue clapboard house with white shutters. And *he* had been in love with Graham's grandmother!

She picked up the letter again, and read the ending:

> These are for your eyes only. I do not think they should be destroyed, but preserved. After all, they are part of our family history, and a hundred years from now they will tell a poignant story of two brave, young lovers who put duty and honor before selfish desire.

Avril slipped Aunt Laura's letter back in its envelope and reached into the trunk. Inside, in an oblong enameled box, she found a packet of letters, tied with a frayed blue ribbon that was faded almost to white.

She got up stiffly from her cramped position and went over closer to the window where the light was better. One by one, she read the letters.

From outside, filtering into her consciousness, came the sound of children playing in the next yard. From somewhere in the house, Avril could hear Gemma and Dorsey, the two maids, chaffing and laughing as they went about the tasks she had given them before coming upstairs. Avril shook off the sense of unreality, immersed as she was in the past as she read Robert's letters to Noramary.

She wiped the tears that had blurred the final lines of the last letter. Then she carefully folded them and replaced them in the little enameled box. There they would stay. Maybe, someday, years from now, someone else would find them and tell Noramary and Robert's love story.

"Avril!" A man's voice broke into her reverie.

Avril jumped up and ran to the top of the attic stairs. Looking down, she saw Logan standing at the foot.

"Logan! What are you doing here?" she gasped.

"Home for Christmas!" he replied. "At

least, that's what I intended to do. Then, when I rode over to Montclair, I heard you had come to Williamsburg, so I thought I'd spend the holidays in town instead."

"How splendid!" Gathering her skirts about her, Avril started down the steps. Catching her hands, Logan bent over and brushed a kiss on her cheek. "This will make Christmas really merry," Avril smiled up at him. "But I didn't know you'd be in Virginia and I don't have a present for you," she said in sudden dismay.

"Being with you again is present enough for me!" Behind the twinkle in his eyes, Avril saw something she had never expected to see. Something that made her draw in her breath in sweet surprise.

Was it possible? Or was she still caught up in the romantic spell of the love letters she had just read? She and Logan, like Noramary and Robert, were childhood friends. Could love happen to her again? But what better basis for love than friendship? Love based on mutual trust, respect, loyalty.

Impossible? Only time would tell, Avril mused, and taking Logan's arm they went the rest of the way downstairs together.

The roll of the drum cracked through the

frosty night air, followed by the piping of the fifes announcing the start of one of the most anticipated Williamsburg Christmas traditions, the Grand Illumination.

In every window of every wreath-bedecked house, winking like a thousand fireflies, candles glowed. Along the streets, crowds had gathered in a spirit of joyous anticipation.

Bundled up warmly against the winter chill, Avril, Logan, Sara, Clay, and the children hurried out of the Barnwell house at the first sound of music. Clay hoisted Bryce onto his shoulders so the little fellow could see over the heads of people pushing for good viewing along the road. Logan lifted Malcolm to a similar vantage point.

Bonfires burned at each corner, and people waiting for the beginning of the annual militia march huddled around them, putting out their hands to absorb the warmth. Flaming cressets on posts lighted the parade route.

"When will it start?" Bryce asked.

"Soon!" replied Clay, his breath making a small silver plume in the cold air.

The stirring music grew louder, and light from the torches could at last be seen, their bright sparks flying into the dark December sky.

"Here they come!" someone shouted, and the militia, their bright uniforms as red as their noses, rounded the corner. In smart formation, they advanced to the cheers of the people standing alongside.

The familiar old carol, played on the sharp notes of dozens of fifes, rang out "Joy to the world, the Lord is come!" accompanied by the rhythmic deep thrumming of the drums. As the members of the militia went by, they were followed by well-wishers and merry-makers, swinging their lanterns on their way to the Christmas proclamation to be read by the governor in front of Government House.

"More! More!" cried Bryce, beating his small fists upon his father's shoulders.

"That's all, son. The soldiers have gone!" Clay told him.

"No! No!" Bryce began to howl.

"For heaven's sake, Clay, let's go inside!" urged Sara.

"We're going to have cranberry punch and cookies, darling," soothed Avril, patting the little boy comfortingly.

"No! I want to see the soldiers!" Bryce protested, and Clay whirled around and began to trot back to the house, bouncing the child playfully.

"That boy!" Sara shook her head. "So determined to have his own way! I declare. Malcolm isn't a bit like that. Where in the world Bryce gets his stubbornness, I don't know!"

Logan squeezed Avril's hand, but they did not dare exchange a knowing glance.

Inside, in the dining room, awaited a delicious feast. Becca, who had accompanied the family to Williamsburg, immediately took Bryce and set him down to tackle a plate piled high with his favorite foods, while the adults moved into the parlor to warm themselves before a glowing fire and sip on hot mulled cider.

Avril had kept all Aunt Laura's Yuletide customs. The Barnwell house was festive with artful decorations. The mantlepiece was draped with greens, and at each window were a wreath and lighted crimson candle. For the dining room table she had fashioned a centerpiece of waxy magnolia leaves, shiny red apples, and pinecones. Burning bayberry candles scented all the rooms with a spicy-sweet fragrance.

When they gathered for the feast — creamed oysters, roast pheasant brought in from Montclair, two bottles of wine made from the famous scuppernong grapes, sweet potatoes, and minted rice — the conversation was congenial and relaxed.

"It's a treat to be here, but I shall have to leave to go back to Montclair for Christmas Day," Clay reminded them. "I wouldn't want to disappoint our people by delaying *their* celebration."

It was a tradition that on Christmas Day the field hands as well as the house servants gathered at the big house for the distribution of gifts from the master, after which a three-day respite from their usual chores was declared.

"Then, I think we should have *our* family Christmas on Christmas Eve, don't you?" Sara asked. "The children would be devastated if you weren't here to see them open their gifts."

"We could attend the Christmas Eve candlelight service at church instead of the one on Christmas morning," Avril suggested. "If you left at dawn, Clayborn, you could be home by early afternoon, couldn't you?"

"A hard ride, Aunt Avril, but I could make it," agreed Clay. "And worth the effort not to miss Christmas here with all of you." He cast a special glance in Sara's direction.

When the fig pudding and fruitcake were brought in and placed on the handsome sideboard to be served later, Logan called for the glasses to be refilled.

"And now I would like to propose a toast," he said.

"Hear! hear!" the rest chimed in, raising their glasses.

"As we all know, the Montrose and Cameron families have been friends for generations. Our ancestors together cut through the wilderness that was once Virginia, built their homes, reared their children, tilled the land, and brought in good harvests. They have endured the hardships of pioneer days, and to paraphrase Scripture — have come into the good land and been richly blessed by the Almighty." He smiled.

The listeners signaled their applause by tapping with their silver on the polished table.

"So, now I want to announce a further, closer alliance between these two families."

Logan gazed at Avril with such intense affection that Sara instinctively turned to look at Clay's aunt. She was startled to see Avril blushing. Her face, in the candlelight, seemed as youthfully radiant as a girl's.

Logan rose and stood behind Avril's chair, one hand resting on her shoulder, the other lifting his glass high as he spoke. "I am overjoyed to say that this lovely lady has done me the singular honor of accepting my proposal of marriage."

As soon as his words were out, Clay pushed back his chair and rushed around the table to pump Logan's hand and embrace Avril.

Sara rose, too, and waiting her turn to congratulate the couple, was dismayed to feel a tiny pang of envy. Why? Didn't she, too, have the love of a good man? In fact, did she not have everything any woman could reasonably expect, or hope for?

Only Sara knew there was something missing. But what?

"Now, it's my turn to make a toast," Clay was saying. "To Avril and Logan, much happiness and many years ahead to share it. And for all of us, may 1843 be the happiest any of us will ever know!"

Savannah
1843

chapter 13

The December day was mild, with only a light wind blowing, when Sara descended the gangplank of the paddle-wheel passenger boat that had brought her from Norfolk to Savannah. She saw the Leighton carriage at once. Standing beside it was the forlorn figure of her father's coachman, Raleigh.

He held his high-topped hat to his chest, baring his gray head as he bowed to Sara and assisted her into the carriage. From his expression Sara feared the worst, and when they drew up in front of the house she saw the door heavily draped in black crepe and hung with a wreath of amaranth leaves tied with a purple ribbon. Her worst fear was confirmed; she had arrived too late to see her father alive.

For a minute Sara closed her eyes, pressing her clasped hands to her breast as if to absorb the pain. Scenes of her father flashed through her mind in rapid impressions. Memories of how as a tiny girl he had tossed her up in his arms, holding her above his head while she laughed with joy. Later memories of his bringing home her first pony and lifting her into the saddle. She remembered how he had gathered his two daughters into his big arms and held them while he wept and told them their mother had gone to heaven. And after that sad time, how he had taken his motherless children to church, on walks, on trips to visit their grandmother in South Carolina.

Sara had begun to understand how lonely Leonard Leighton's life must have been until he met and married the pretty young widow, Georgina Nugent. Perhaps if she had understood earlier, she might not have been so hostile, made things so difficult when Georgina came into their household.

Well, the past is past; she thought with her characteristic practicality. *And nothing can be done about the mistakes that were made.*

The door of the carriage opened. Gathering herself together, she got out and braced herself to enter the house where her father's vigorous personality was no longer present.

Trent, his eyes watery and red-rimmed,

opened the door for her and she stepped inside.

"Mournful day, Miss Sara," he said. "Mastuh done passed over. Mahty sad time."

He took the cape she handed him and Sara untied her bonnet strings. The interior of the hall was unnaturally dark, a darkness created by the drawn draperies, customary in a house where death has occurred.

As Sara stood there, orienting herself both to the oppressive silence and the realization of her loss, she heard a voice from the stairway and looked up to see Lucie leaning over the banister of the second-floor balcony.

"Oh, Sara, I'm so glad you're here!"

"Lucie!" She hurried to the foot of the stairs while Lucie made her way carefully down.

The sisters embraced tearfully, then Sara stepped back and gave her an appraising look. "You're looking wonderfully well, Lucie, in spite of everything. When is the baby due?"

Lucie's cheeks flushed and she smiled. Then, as if she thought it not proper to evidence any sign of happiness under their sorrowful circumstances, she lowered her voice. "In March. Oh Sara, it is so sad Papa did not live to see my child. I wanted so much to give Papa a grandson!"

"He had two grandsons in Virginia," Sara reminded her sharply. It was still a bitter pill for Sara that her father had never traveled to Montclair to see either Malcolm or Bryce. Nor had Georgina ever invited her to bring the children for a visit when Papa was alive.

Lucie's eyes filled with tears. "I know, Sara. I'm sorry. I didn't mean to imply —" she amended, "I just meant here in Savannah where he could see them often, watch them grow up —"

Immediately Sara was contrite. "Don't worry, Lucie." She put her arm around the younger woman's shoulders.

"I intend to call the baby — if it is a boy — Leonard," Lucie confided shyly.

"That's lovely, Lucie. I know Papa would have been very pleased," Sara said. Inwardly, she wondered if her father might have been hurt that *she* had not named her firstborn son after him. Could that be the reason he had made no effort to travel to Montclair to see Malcolm? After all, Malcolm was the *first* grandchild.

But at the time of his son's birth Clay wanted to follow the Montrose tradition of using the strong Scottish names given most males in the family, and she had consented.

It was only now she wondered how this decision might have affected her father.

When her second son was born, she had followed a custom in her mother's family and given him Emma's maiden name, Bryson.

Well, it was too late for regrets. What was done was done. There was no making up for things she had overlooked. It would only cause more grief in the long run.

"How is Georgina?" Sara felt forced to ask. She had no real desire to see her stepmother. It always put her on the defensive, for she could not pretend an affection she did not feel. But duty and correct behavior had been instilled in her from so early an age, that behaving properly came as second nature.

"She's holding up remarkably well," Lucie told her. "Scott and Bowen have been sent for and should be arriving any time now."

"Should I go up and see her?" asked Sara, feeling her own reluctance.

"She's resting, Sara. She had a bad night. Camella is with her. She'll let us know when Georgina wakes up."

Sara was ashamed at the relief she felt in being granted a reprieve, at least for a little while. She dreaded the ordeal of facing her stepmother after all these years. They had never been friends, would never be. It was useless to think that this mutual sorrow would make them so.

"Well, then, let's have Trent bring us some coffee and you can tell me about everything," Sara suggested.

The drawing room was closed and would not be open until after the memorial service for the reception of family and friends making formal condolence calls. So the sisters went into the small parlor that had been their father's private sanctuary. As they walked in, both felt a fresh assault of painful memories.

When Sara asked about her father's illness, Lucie filled in the details of his last days.

"He was stricken in his office at the Cotton Exchange, but recovered sufficiently to be brought home in his own carriage. Georgina says he walked into the house unassisted, complained of feeling rather unwell, then collapsed. Dr. Lefevre says the second stroke was more severe. At first they thought his paralysis and speech impairment would be temporary." Lucie's eyes brimmed with tears again, and she took out her tiny pocket handkerchief and wiped them. "Then Papa lapsed into a coma and

— as you know — never fully regained consciousness."

"Not once? Didn't he ever recognize you, Lucie, nor mention me?" asked Sara, the emotion in her voice revealing how much she longed to hear that in the moments of lucidity her father might have thought of her, wished her by his side, spoken lovingly of his eldest daughter.

Lucie placed both her hands over her sister's clenched ones. "I'm sorry, Sara. I sat by his bed for hours at a time, relieving Georgina and Camella, and I talked to him. But Papa never indicated he knew me . . . and he never answered."

Sara struggled to hide the hurt she felt. She had idolized her father, been fiercely jealous of Georgina's usurping what she had always considered her special place with Leonard. Now, he was gone without a word to her, a moment of farewell she could cherish and treasure for the rest of her life.

"We must remember the happy times, Sara," Lucie counseled gently.

When Trent brought in the tray with the silver coffee server and a plate of thin lemon wafers, Sara served them both and sipped her cup silently until she felt somewhat revived. Then the conversation took a lighter turn, with Lucie asking about her small nephews. Sara noted fondly that, as a mother-to-be herself, her sister was showing great interest in the children's development.

"You must come to Virginia with the baby in the fall, Lucie. I'm sure Brock will permit it, won't he?" Sara herself had no doubt her mild mannered brother-in-law would put up no objection to anything Lucie wanted to do. "Malcolm and Bryce would be so thrilled to see you again. They still talk about the games you played with them."

"I'd love that. To me, Montclair is a perfect paradise."

There was a discreet knock on the door and when Sara acknowledged it, Camella, Georgina's personal maid, entered. She dropped a slight curtsy before greeting Sara.

"Miss Georgina asks y'all to come upstairs now, Miss Lucie."

Sara and Lucie exchanged a glance — one, signifying her disinclination; the other, encouragement. They rose and followed Camella up the broad, curving stairway to their stepmother's darkened room.

Georgina rested on a small mountain of lace-trimmed satin pillows, monogrammed with her initials. She was wearing a loose gown of black velvet edged with cascades of black Valenciennes lace.

Sara wondered how her stepmother had managed to have such an elegant mourning gown made within the short time she had been a widow. A matter of days, actually. Had she anticipated her husband's death in such a calculated way as to make arrangements with a dressmaker to fit and complete the garments even before Leonard Leighton died?

Even as the thought crossed her mind, Sara rebuked herself. Repentant, she started across the room to where Georgina reclined on a curved back chaise.

Her stepmother's narrow face, although fine of feature, wore a faintly discontented expression, the mouth drawn down in a look of perpetual petulance. She offered her cheek now for Sara's dutiful kiss, then motioned them both to sit down.

"Well, Sara, it is a sad day indeed that you have at last come, and too late to bid your father a last farewell," Georgina began.

Sara checked a bitter retort. Instead, she said coldly, "The fact is, I did not receive word that he was even ill until he had been unconscious three days. I came as fast as I could travel." She could feel Lucie's body stiffening with tension.

Determined not to cause any discomfort to anyone, especially not her beloved sister,

Sara stopped short of screaming, *My father dearly loved me! It was you, Georgina, who drove a wedge of misunderstanding between us all these years!*

Georgina patted her coiffure, and again a wickedly uncharitable thought popped into Sara's mind: *How odd that the grief-stricken widow had enough stamina to sit for hours while her hair was dressed so elaborately.*

As if speaking was a greater effort than should be expected of a recently bereaved woman, Georgina said wearily, "As you both know, complying with your father's request that he be buried in your grandmother's family plot in his home church in South Carolina, the funeral took place there. A very wearying trip, I must say, and in my opinion, unnecessary, since Leonard spent most of his life in Savannah — and since your grandmother is in her eighties and was barely able to attend the services."

"But, of course," Georgina continued, "I always try to accommodate others." Sara fought the almost uncontrollable urge to dart an incredulous glance at Lucie while her stepmother droned on, "So we are having a memorial service here. Leonard's friends will want to pay their respects by calling afterwards. Except for my brief appearance at the service itself, of course, I cannot possibly receive the dozens of guests who will be coming to make condolence calls." Here she fixed Sara with a look of icy intensity. "Since it is unthinkable that Lucie appear in public in her condition, *you,* Sara, must represent the family and receive the guests."

So it was as a concession to her stepmother's directions that Sara came to be standing by herself at the entrance to the drawing room after the long service consisting of verbose eulogies given by her father's longtime friends and business associates. One by one, the guests filed by, pressing her hand and uttering expressions of sympathy.

It was all Sara could do to maintain a dignified demeanor and hold in check her own emotions, so very near the surface. Here, alone and vulnerable, she looked up to see him walk through the archway.

As he moved purposefully toward her, Sara felt herself grow cold, as if ice had suddenly replaced the blood in all her veins. Her heart began to pump wildly even as her body seemed to turn to stone. She stood, transfixed, unable to breathe, to move.

She wiped her suddenly clammy palms on the black-bordered handkerchief she held crumpled in her hands, and vainly wished to be safely upstairs with Lucie.

But he pushed on through the guests crowding the narrow hallway until he was only a few feet from her, so close she could see those vivid blue eyes. His face, still tawny, was thinner, so much so that the aquiline features she remembered seemed now sharper, the cheekbones more prominent, and two deep lines now bracketed his mouth. In his eyes was an expression they had never held before.

There was no time for Sara to define it, because Theo was speaking, his voice as mellow and rich as ever. "Sara." He spoke her name like a caress. Bowing over the numb hand she extended, he said, "My sincere sympathy to your stepmother and sister, and to you, Sara, in this time of great sadness."

She tried to withdraw her hand, but he held it while his eyes explored her face. The hand he'd captured lay like a wounded bird in his palm. It must have been only a moment, but to Sara it seemed like an eternity as they looked at one another across the bridge of years.

Then, as if suddenly aware of the people behind him, he straightened. When she tugged gently to disengage her hand, she felt him insert something small, square, and hard; then he closed her fingers over it and released her hand.

"Wonderful to see you again, Sara," he murmured, then moved on, leaving her weak and shaken.

Without looking to see what Theo had written, she thrust the card into the velvet reticule alongside the tiny vial of smelling salts attached to her belt.

There was such a crush of visitors toward the end of the afternoon that Sara could not leave her post, nor did she notice when Theo left. It was only after the last lingering guest had finally taken leave that she had the opportunity to take out the card and read what was written on it.

> Sara, I must see you. For what we once meant to each other, I beg you not to refuse. I will be waiting in the park across from your house every evening at seven until you come. Ever yours. T.

Sara crushed the card as her hands closed convulsively around it. How dare Theo do this? How dare he attempt to rekindle an old flame? With both of them married, he must be out of his mind to suggest such a thing!

Sara realized she was trembling, breathing shallowly. Then she heard

Lucie's voice, and she came slowly out of her reverie of burning memories and unfulfilled dreams.

Hurrying to the foot of the stairs, she looked up. "Yes, Lucie, what is it?"

"If everyone is gone, Stepmama wants you to bring the guest book so she can read the names of those who called."

Stiffly Sara turned, walked over to the hall table, picked up the signed book, and started slowly up the stairs. She felt drained, but tinglingly aware, every one of her senses warning her of impending danger.

chapter 14

Because Georgina was entering a period of formal mourning and because Lucie's advanced pregnancy prohibited her journeying out as well, it was left for Sara to go alone to the stonecutter to make arrangements for their father's grave. But not before selecting an appropriate epitaph to be engraved on it. And there was a lengthy debate as to which verse or quotation might be best.

"Let's go into Papa's study and look through his bookshelves," Lucie finally suggested. "Maybe we can find something that meant a great deal to him. He might have had a favorite book of poetry."

"Poetry? Papa?" Sara had rarely seen their father read anything but the financial pages of the daily newspaper.

"You never know. We've got to start somewhere, Sara," Lucie said practically.

Walking into Leonard's study was evocative of everything they remembered about their father. Sara had often been called into this room to be reprimanded for some fall from grace. But there were happier memories as well. The two little girls had come here often, after their mother died, to play quietly with their dolls or Noah's ark while Leonard read the paper. There were other special moments when he had held them on his lap and told them stories about his country boyhood in South Carolina, quail hunting, or fishing in the stream that ran through the Leighton property there.

Both sisters felt a poignant wave of nostalgia as they looked about and saw his leather armchair, the desk with its green glass shade and the globe of the world on its wooden stand that, as children, they had spun around and around.

Nothing seemed to have been moved or disturbed in here since the morning Leonard had left for his Cotton Exchange office and returned, stricken with the illness that would prove fatal.

They moved quietly around the room, Lucie taking book after book from the shelves, turning pages, pausing to read something. Sara examined the contents of the square walnut desk. As she opened the right-hand drawer, she saw a well-worn Bible and gave a little exclamation.

"Look at this, Lucie," she said, holding it

up for her sister's inspection.

Together they read the inscription on the flyleaf: "To my dear son, Leonard, in the hope that he will make the daily reading of God's Word a part of his life. Your mother, Lavelle Leighton."

Sara thumbed through the pages, many of them dog-eared and filled with underlining. Looking up from this discovery, they exchanged a significant glance.

Then they paused at one page in Isaiah where, in their father's handwriting, they read this notation: "Read at Mother's funeral. To be engraved on her headstone."

"Well, what do you think?" Sara asked after a moment's silence.

"Yes," Lucie said simply, and Sara dipped the desk pen into the inkwell and began to copy the lines.

That was the slip of paper she handed Kenneth Cartwright, the stonecutter, when she arrived at his studio-workshop.

"We want a carving of a spreading live oak tree with hanging Spanish moss and then . . . this," she explained.

He read it aloud to be sure he had it correct.

> No more will the sun give you daylight

Nor the moonlight shine on you,
But the Lord will be your everlasting
light.
Your God will be your splendor.

Isaiah 60:19

Sara felt the hard lump swell in her throat as she listened to the words and had difficulty conducting the rest of the necessary business arrangements without giving way to tears.

When she left Cartwright's Stoneworks and started toward the carriage, her head was bowed, the mourning veil on her bonnet covering her face.

"Sara!" she heard a voice call.

Recognizing it, she halted. A man's caped figure stepped out from behind the shaggy bushes next to the building and Sara froze, rooted to the spot. *It was Theo.*

"Sara —" The voice was hypnotic, mesmerizing. She felt like an insect in a web, with the spider closing in for the kill, but still she could not move. "I have to speak to you. We must talk."

Alarmed by the intensity of his voice, Sara replied, "We have nothing to say!" and started toward the carriage. But Theo was quicker and cut off her approach.

To detain her, he put out a restraining

hand. "Listen, Sara, there may never be another opportunity."

Frantic, she tried to wrest herself free of his grasp, but he would not let her go. His voice was low and soothing as he pleaded, "Sara, I've waited every evening across the street from your house, in the dark, cold, the rain — waiting, desperately hoping you would overcome your aversion, your fear — whatever it is that keeps you from coming."

"How dare you —"

"I dare," he cut in, "because my very sanity depends upon it." His fingers tightened on her arm. "Please! All I ask is that you hear me out. Let me explain what has burdened me all these years. Can you not spare me a few minutes of your time?"

Sara could think of no way to escape his vise-like grip without risking a scene. Several passersby had already glanced in their direction, curious as to the confrontation taking place. Sara felt trapped.

She saw that Raleigh, the Leightons' coachman, was standing beside the carriage, ready to open the door for her. Impulsively, Sara made a decision. It would be better to talk inside the carriage, shielded from curious eyes, than to stand out here on the street in plain view of the townspeople. She could not chance someone who knew them spotting them together, suspecting it was an arranged rendezvous.

"Come then," she said tensely, motioning with her free hand toward the carriage.

Theo loosened his hold, but kept his hand firmly on her arm as he escorted her to the carriage and assisted her inside.

In the enclosed intimacy of the interior of the coach, Sara almost panicked. What had she been thinking? This was a mistake. But it was too late. Wiser to let Theo have his say, then end this episode as quickly as possible.

Theo gazed at her with something in his expression that stirred her very soul. What was it — remorse, regret, longing, supplication? Her hands clenched into such tight fists that had it not been for her black kid gloves, the nails would have cut the tender flesh.

Now that they were alone, Theo seemed to be having trouble speaking what was on his mind. He took a deep breath. "Please remove your veil, Sara. It is more difficult to talk through it, and there have been too many barriers between us for too long. I want to see you when I say what I have to say."

With shaky hands, Sara lifted her veil.

"How lovely you are, Sara," he whispered. "You have scarcely changed."

She straightened her shoulders. "You're wrong, Theo," she said, her tone cold. "I have changed a great deal. I am no longer the foolish, infatuated girl you duped into believing you loved her."

Theo shook his head. "Sara, if you only knew how many times I have castigated myself for the hurt I caused you. The circumstances were such that it was impossible to tell you my reasons without injuring someone else — someone who did not deserve anything but kindness and consideration."

"I suppose you mean Evangeline Archer," Sara said reproachfully. The moment the name slipped out, she was sorry. She had not meant to show any reaction during this talk Theo had forced upon her, nor give him any idea of the agony she had experienced over their broken romance. Her only intent was to let Theo speak his mind, then dismiss him haughtily from her presence . . . and her life.

"It's true," he agreed sadly. "I could not bring myself to be that cruel."

"But you did not hesitate to be cruel to *me!*" she retorted.

"Sara, you are so strong. I knew you would soon recover from whatever hurt I inflicted. There were a dozen others standing in line for a glance or gesture from you! As a matter of fact, almost every young man in Savannah was in love with you!"

"So that is your justification for callously leading me on, then brutally telling me of your engagement to someone else?" she flung at him with all her old fire. "How did you know that I was not as capable of suffering as anyone else?"

"Sara, you *have* survived. You are more beautiful than ever. I can see new strength and character in your face, your bearing. I watched you with your father's guests at the memorial service, your dignity, your graciousness — all that is new."

"That may be true. But it still does not explain nor excuse you for what you did to me." She was adamant. The emotions she had dammed up all these years were, in spite of her resolve, ready to spill out. She found herself wanting to hurt Theo as he had hurt her. This was her chance for revenge. Perhaps the only chance she would ever have. "I loved you! I would have given up everything for you! Didn't I offer to run away with you and forfeit the lavish wedding my family would have given us? What more could any man want? Has what you gave *me* up for been worth it to you?" she demanded.

For a moment Theo seemed taken aback by her outburst. He regarded her flashing eyes, the high color burning in her cheeks.

"Sara, I never meant to be cruel to you. J thought I was being kind. If I had followed my heart's desire, eloped with you, forsaken my family, my responsibility, and yes, my honor — it would have been the cruelest thing I could have done to the person I loved most in the world. *You, Sara!* If we had run away together, you would have come to hate me for ruining your life."

She stared at him, unable to follow the gist of his meaning.

"Your life has turned out well, hasn't it, Sara? You are married to a fine man. You have children, haven't you?"

"Yes. Two boys . . . but I don't see what that has —" This whole encounter was unreal, bizarre. She and Theo, after all these years.

"You see," he went on, as if explaining the alphabet to a very young child, "sometimes things turn out for the best. Ironically, most often they do. Doesn't even Scripture tell us that 'everything works together for good for those who love the Lord and are called to His purpose'? How can we ever be sure what His purpose is in the things that happen to us in life? Perhaps your purpose was to marry Clayborn Montrose and mother his children. And mine? Well, unfortunately, I have not yet discovered His purpose in mine." Theo sighed heavily.

"I must go, Theo," Sara said. All her old feelings, the old anguish of his rejection threatened to rise disturbingly, and she knew it was dangerous to linger here alone with him any longer.

Her hands were still imprisoned in his, and he leaned forward, saying huskily, "Sara, Sara, the nights I have lain awake thinking of you, dreaming of you, longing for you — to hold you — kiss you —"

Frightened, Sara drew back. "No, Theo, this is wrong. You must go," she said firmly. Inside, she was trembling, feeling her pulses race, knowing how close she was to temptation. "Please! If you have any love left for me, go now, before we do something foolish that we will both regret."

"Ah, Sara, Sara!" moaned Theo. For a minute his face twisted in the agony of desire, regret, and relinquishment. "What did I always tell you? You *are* strong. I am not. What a fool I was to let you go. I will never get over losing you. You were . . . *are* . . . the love of my life."

Then, before she could stop him, Theo had pulled her into his arms and kissed her.

It was a kiss full of tenderness, passion, and finally, renunciation. When it ended, Sara could not speak.

Theo released her gently. "Good bye, Sara. I will never try to see you nor contact you again. I promise. I just needed to let you know I loved you. I loved you the first time I saw you. I love you still. I will go on loving you for the rest of my life."

Theo opened the carriage door, stepped out, then turned and looked back at Sara for an endless moment. "Forgive me, Sara," he said and closed the door.

Sara slumped back against the leather cushions, shuddering.

Suddenly she heard the sound of glass against metal as Raleigh opened the pass-through from the driver's seat. "You wants go home now, Miss Sara?"

"Yes," she replied, knowing Raleigh meant the Leighton house. But Sara realized that she really longed to go home to Montclair — to Clay and her children.

chapter 15

The day Sara left Savannah, the weather turned dreary. Gray clouds hovering overhead added to her sense of desolation. As her small trunk was placed on top of the carriage that was to take her to the dock, Sara had the strange premonition she would never return to this house.

Her father was dead, and she had no reason to believe Georgina would ever invite her back. And why should she even want to come? Lucie and her husband lived in the country miles from town, where they had built their own beautiful house. If Sara should ever need to come to Savannah, she was sure of a welcome there.

Still, this house held memories that could not be laid to rest as easily as her father's body had been planted in the soil of South Carolina.

The evening before, the sisters had talked far into the night. They had discussed the fact that neither of them would receive any inheritance from their father's estate. By a recent change in Leonard's will, everything had come to Georgina, and she had been quite blunt about it, stating that since both were married to wealthy men, they needed nothing more from her. But it was a bitter pill to swallow that she had not at least offered them the opportunity to select something of sentimental value to take away with them from their father's home.

"It's so like her," Sara said bitterly. "Selfish, inconsiderate, insensitive!"

"It doesn't matter," consoled Lucie. "They're only *things.* We still have each other and the memory of the good times when we were children. And she *is* right that we are both blessed with good husbands who will see that we lack for nothing."

When it was time for her to leave, Sara said a final goodbye to her stepmother with all the cool detachment that had always marked their relationship. But parting with Lucie brought inevitable sadness. Both knew that, when they left this house, they would be bidding farewell to their childhood once and for all, the girlish dreams they had dreamed together, the hopes for the future they had shared.

As she hugged Lucie, Sara reminded her, "If you need me when the baby comes, you have only to send word."

"Thank you, Sara, but Brock's mother will be there and, of course, Mammy June is now with us, too."

Even this reasonable refusal caused Sara pain. Lucie had a life of her own, comfortable and happy, and there was little room in it for Sara. Though she was gratified for her sister, this was yet another door that was closing to her. She shook off the feeling of depression and gave Lucie a bright smile, promising to visit "soon."

Tying on her bonnet, Sara fastened the braid clasps of her cape and, with a final embrace, hurried down the stone steps to the carriage waiting to take her to the dock.

Before going below to the shelter of her cabin, Sara stood on deck as the boat maneuvered its way out of the harbor cluttered with ships loaded with cargo. A light rain had begun to fall, and the farther they moved into the channel leading out to sea, the more blurred grew the outline of the buildings along the wharves below the bluff.

A sense of finality enveloped Sara, and she shivered involuntarily. This had been so sorrowful a journey in every way that she felt deadly cold, riddled with inconsolable grief and lingering regrets.

Gathering her cloak around her, she

turned away before the shoreline was completely out of sight, and went below.

When she reached her cabin, she was chilling so violently that Lizzie, who had accompanied her mistress to Savannah, wrapped her in blankets and brought her hot tea.

"You must have cotched sumpin', Miz Sara. You jest done too much de whole time we been gone. Traipsin' 'round in de chill, doin' all de honors fo' Miz Leighton." Lizzie shook her head as she fussed over Sara.

Sara let her fuss. Lizzie might think she was coming down with something, but Sara knew better. Huddled in the comfort Lizzie was providing her, Sara allowed her mind to wander over the events of the recent past. Perhaps, once in every life, a person is able to see herself as she really is, stripped of all pretense. That day it happened to Sara.

The unanticipated encounter with Theo thrust itself vividly into her consciousness, and she relived it in all its horrifying reality. Although she had not actually arranged it, was it possible that, by her secret thoughts, she had somehow brought it about? How many hours had she spent fantasizing about just such a meeting? Over and over she had rehearsed what she would say, what she would do if ever she had the opportunity to confront Theo with his perfidy. How many years had she entertained secret longings and frustrated dreams of what "might have been"?

With a shudder of revulsion, Sara buried her face in her hands, knowing it was all true.

In the cold light of reality, Sara had to admit she had been flattered that Theo had never forgotten her, that even after all these years, he still loved her. He had confessed to tormenting thoughts of her and regrets that he had given her up. Wasn't that what she really wanted? Theo's declaration of undying love? To know that she still held the upper hand, that he had not rejected her, after all?

Sara groaned. Oh, how wicked she was! She was guilty of pride! She had been taught that pride is one of the seven deadly sins. Now she could no longer deny that she had clung to her guilty love for Theo out of pride, allowing it to poison her marriage, her appreciation for the fine man who was now her husband.

That love had haunted her waking and sleeping hours like some evil thing. She had foolishly nurtured her heartbreak, deifying it as something noble, writhing in anguish over losing him, harboring bitterness for the woman who had taken him from her.

Sara was ashamed. She felt ugly, blemished, degraded as she saw herself, unadorned. What was it the Bible said about such sin? Wasn't even the thought of someone other than your spouse considered adultery?

Oh, dear God, forgive me! Sara cried from her heart.

At last she saw clearly what a twisted thing love could become. Now, with all the honesty and integrity of which the new Sara was capable, she faced this demon within, and exorcised it.

chapter 16

In Williamsburg a light snow powdered the ground while great, puffy snowdrops floated lackadaisically from a cloud-heavy sky.

Clayborn Montrose, pacing back and forth impatiently, waited in front of the Raleigh Inn for Sara's arrival by stage from Norfolk. After her absence of nearly a month, Clay was as anxious as a bridegroom to see his wife again.

This beautiful, enigmatic woman still intrigued him, fascinated him with her beauty, her mystery, her mercurial personality. He often marveled at his incredible good fortune in convincing her to marry him. He had done everything in his power to make her happy. But after nearly seven years, he was still not sure he had succeeded.

He saw her before she saw him, and he drew in his breath. Sara had never worn black before and, although it was her badge of mourning, it enhanced her beauty as he had never seen it. Like a beautiful jewel set against black velvet, her face in its pallor had a luminous quality. The eyes, shadowed now with fatigue from her travels and the grueling schedule of her father's last rites, were so dark blue that they appeared almost purple.

She was giving Lizzie directions about her baggage, so was not aware of Clay's approach until he called her name. At this, she spun around with a cry of welcome that thrilled his heart.

"Oh, Clay, darling, I'm so happy to see you!"

"And I *you,* dearest. Was the trip exhausting?" he asked solicitously. "I've brought the carriage. The horses are fed and ready to go . . . unless you would like to remain overnight in Williamsburg and leave tomorrow morning after a good night's rest."

"No, no, Clay. I'd like to start at once. I'm anxious to get home. How are the boys?"

"Fine. But I had a hard time dissuading Malcolm from insisting on coming with me to meet you. They have missed you, my dear." Clay smiled fondly at Sara, then added in a lower tone, "As have I! More than I can tell you." He took her hand, and slipping it through his arm, covered it with his other one, gazing down at her with hungry eyes.

By the time they had transferred Sara's baggage to the Montrose carriage and had Lizzie settled in the enclosed driver's seat in front beside Joshua, it had begun to snow heavily.

"Warm enough?" Clay asked Sara once they were seated, tucking the fur-lined lap robe more securely around her.

"Yes, thank you."

Peering out the carriage window at the changing landscape, Sara admired the lacy frosting on trees, housetops, and lantern posts. "How beautiful it is!" she exclaimed.

But by the time they turned onto the road leading out of town, familiar landmarks were rapidly fading, obliterated by the falling snow. The whole countryside appeared suspended in time. Even the clop-clop of the horses' hooves was muffled by the white blanket, and the carriage proceeded as if by magic, transported by flying steeds on billowy clouds.

Sara was too relieved to be with Clay again to notice much about the world outside their window. As they rode along, he answered her questions about the children's activities since she had been away. Avril and

Logan had been back for a brief visit before leaving for Natchez, where Logan was completing all the legalities concerning the sale of the Dumont property there for Avril.

"They were sorry to have missed seeing you, and I'm sure Aunt Avril wrote you how deeply sorry she was about your father's death."

"Yes, a beautiful letter, full of love and sympathy," replied Sara.

"You know they will be leaving for Jamaica from New Orleans without returning to Virginia?"

"I'd forgotten. I've had so many things on my mind."

"Understandable, of course."

"And how long will they be gone?"

"Logan wasn't sure. I suppose it depends on the size of his holdings. You do remember my telling you that he has been retained by an old schoolmate at the English school they attended together as boys, to settle his father's Jamaican plantation estate, don't you?" Clay turned an inquiring gaze on Sara, and she smiled wearily, shrugging her shoulders. "Well, at any rate they will be staying in one of the guest houses on the plantation while they're there. Logan has visited before and says the way of life on the islands is most pleasant — a lovely place to spend the winter, he says." At this, Clay paused to look out the window. "And speaking of winter — it seems as though we're in for a snowy one. We've had a few flurries, but none that looked like this!"

The pace of the horses had slowed and the carriage moved more tentatively now. Roads already deeply rutted by heavy fall rains were glazing over as the snow continued to fall.

For the next few minutes both husband and wife gazed out at the scene. Sara's thoughts were of Avril and how love had come into her life a second time with the gentle sweetness of an old and cherished friendship. Avril and Logan had been married in a quiet ceremony in the little chapel built at Montclair by Graham at Avril's request long ago. "Love suffereth long and is kind; love envieth not; love doth not behave itself unseemly; seeketh not her own; . . . beareth all things, believeth all things, hopeth all things, endureth all things. Love never faileth" — the words from Avril and Logan's ceremony brought back the meaning of that day.

That was ideal love. An ideal to be strived for, if not attained. How lacking she had been in all those attributes.

She glanced over at Clay, felt a pang of remorse, knowing that she had failed to give him the fullest expression of her love in holding on to one forbidden, lost to her forever. What folly! How could she make up to Clay all the years she had wasted, yearning after something and someone who, in the end had proved worthless?

"Whoa!" they heard Joshua shout, and the carriage lurched, rocked unsteadily, then halted abruptly.

Clay frowned and opened the carriage door. "What's the trouble?" he shouted to the coachman.

"Snowdrifts, suh. Pretty deep out here. I missed de turn into Montclair gates, dat's all. I'm gettin' down to lead the horse around and back."

Clay had to struggle to shut the door again, tugging to wrest it from the strong wind that sent whirls of snow into the carriage.

Sara leaned forward to try to see out the snow-blurred window. "I've never seen anything like this!" she exclaimed excitedly. "Is this a blizzard?"

"Not really. But it's quite a heavy storm. I wonder —" he paused thoughtfully. "Perhaps I should check Eden Cottage before we go up to the house."

At Sara's look of surprise, Clay explained,

"I ought to be sure all the windows are securely fastened, the doors bolted. This wind could play havoc if there is a loosely hooked window or door left unlatched.

"I sent Dorsey down to clean and straighten everything after Aunt Avril left," he continued, "but I'd feel better if I made sure myself. There are so many family heirlooms there, things Aunt Avril treasures. I'd hate to see them ruined —" There was a note of apology in his tone.

"Well, of course, Clay," Sara assured him. "Do whatever needs to be done."

"Then I'll tell Joshua we're stopping." Clay pushed open the door again, leaned out, and shouted the order to the coachman. Pulling the door shut once more, he brushed snow off his shoulders. "It must have been snowing harder and longer out here than in Williamsburg. It's already quite deep."

"What fun the children will have!" Sara smiled, her eyes sparkling.

Clayborn felt his heart lift. Sara had seemed so pensive, so withdrawn since her arrival. It was good to see a flicker of her usual vivaciousness again.

The carriage came to a stop in front of Eden Cottage, built as the architect's model for Montclair. Within the family, it was called the "honeymoon house," since traditionally this was where most Montrose newlyweds spent their first year of marriage. Of course, when Clay and Sara were married, the reverse was true. It was Avril who had moved from the big house into this smaller cottage.

As he started to get out, Clay said, "I won't be long."

"Wait, Clay. I want to come with you!"

He hesitated. "It will be cold, my dear. The place has been empty over a week and no fires burning —"

"I don't care. I want to come," she insisted.

He looked down at her fine leather boots with their delicate high French heels. "Your feet will get soaked in those —" he said doubtfully. "Oh, well, come, I'll carry you."

She placed her hands on his shoulders, and he lifted her easily into his arms. She laughed lightly as he tramped through the snow onto the tiny porch. Still holding her, he reached for the door handle and the door swung open.

With Sara still in his arms, Clay stepped inside.

"I feel like a bride being carried over the threshold!" she exclaimed gaily.

He set her on her feet. "I'll have a quick

look around and then we can be on our way," he told her and started to the back of the house.

Sara stood looking around. She had always loved coming to visit Avril here, although those times had been few. Avril usually came to Montclair and brought the little boys back to Eden Cottage for tea parties or special treats.

Everything in the cottage reflected her touch. There was not a false note anywhere. Avril had maintained the integrity of the original, keeping the Colonial furnishings, most of them made by Montclair's plantation artisans right on the land, and a few authentic antiques brought by Claire Montrose, Duncan's mother, from her home in Scotland. Avril, though, had also placed her own individual stamp on the place.

There was her artist's easel standing in the alcove by the window where she could get the best north light. On the wall were the framed portraits she had done of Graham, of Clayborn when he was a young lad, and of both Malcolm and Bryce. A portfolio lay open on the table nearby, and Sara went over to look through it. As she did, she was surprised to find many sketches of her own children she had never seen, as well as the small black children on the plantation.

She knew that Avril rarely went anywhere without a tiny paintbox, brushes, and sketchbook. Sara had always admired Avril's delicate watercolors of her European travels as well as the many lovely landscapes she did of the meadows and woods around Montclair. She would surely return from Jamaica with more beautiful records of this new adventure in her life.

Sara moved over to a table to examine several objects there. A silver twin-frame held miniatures of a young man and woman costumed in fashions of the past century — Avril's parents perhaps? Next was a small, hand-painted porcelain music box. Sara lifted the lid and immediately the tinkling notes of the minuet filled the room with the musical memories of an earlier time.

There was a lilting quality to the tune, along with an underlying minor theme that evoked the message of love mingled with longing, happiness, and heartbreak. Someday she would have to ask Avril about this exquisite little box. There must be some story connected with it, and Avril knew most of the stories about the brides who had come to Montclair.

Slowly Sara circled the room, sensing something here she needed to experience.

The cottage had an expectant air, as if waiting for its mistress's return. And yet there was a welcoming atmosphere as well, as if it offered its own warmth and loving acceptance to all who entered here. To the right of the front door hung a simple wooden cross on which Avril had done the words in a flowing calligraphy script: *LORD AND MASTER, BLESS AND PROTECT EVERYONE WHO COMES IN OR OUT.*

"Well, everything's fine. Shall we be on our way then?" Clay came striding back into the room.

Sara stood, her back to him, gazing out the window. It was late afternoon now and the approach of winter dusk cast purple shadows upon the snow.

"Clay, let's stay the night here," she suggested softly.

He looked puzzled. "Here? But, darling —"

"I would so like to, Clay. Perhaps it's a whim, but could we? We can send Lizzie and Joshua up to the house, tell them we'll be up in the morning. It will soon be the children's bedtime and if we arrive now, there will be such excitement they will never settle down. Besides," she added almost shyly, "I should like to have some time alone with my husband. Here."

There was a moment of silence as Clay seemed to be weighing the suggestion against some more practical considerations. Then he spoke decisively, "Of course, darling, if that's what you want. There's plenty of firewood, supplies, whatever we need." He went to the door. "You sure you don't want Lizzie to stay?"

Sara shook her head, smiling. "No, just us."

A few minutes later Clay returned with an armload of firewood. "We'll get a fire going and warm this place up," he said heartily.

Sara moved aside so he could arrange the kindling, place the logs, and strike the flint to start the fire. At the first crackle of the wood as it began to catch, Clay rocked back on his heels and replaced the fireguard.

Kneeling side by side in front of the fireplace, Sara looked at Clay, and he was glad to see the old sparkle and laughter in her eyes. *What a lark this is!* they seemed to say.

Soon the flames began leaping, sending out a warming glow from the logs, now burning cheerfully. Sara's face, illumined by the firelight, seemed to Clay lovelier than ever.

Thoughtfully, Sara held out her left hand, twisting the third finger to let the magnificent ruby in her ring catch the light of the fire. As she turned it, the deep crimson stone seemed to burn with an enduring flame. It seemed to symbolize what it represented, that love is eternal.

Sara instinctively turned to gaze at Clay's face, observing the new maturity in the strongly molded features, the added purpose and responsibility in his brown eyes.

An awareness of intimacy trembled between them. The air throbbed with something vital, as if from invisible wings stirring, vibrating with consciousness of each other that was new, different from ever before.

Slowly Clay got to his feet and held out his hands to pull Sara up with him. Together they stepped back from the fireplace. Clay, still holding her hands, raised them to his lips. For a moment they stood looking at each other. Then Sara leaned forward, lifting her head for his kiss. She closed her eyes and felt the world slipping away.

When Sara awakened the next morning, she lay still for a moment, listening to the ice-clad branches of the trees tapping with silvery fingers at the window. The bedroom door was open, and when she turned her head she could see into the parlor where a cheerful fire crackled merrily.

She had no idea what time it was. She was only aware of a deep, peaceful contentment. She had been right to suggest their staying in Eden Cottage last night. It must have been an inspiration. This place was a magical setting for love.

Though she had often wished that she and Clay, like so many other Montrose couples before them, could have lived here in Eden Cottage for the first year of their marriage, she now suspected the time would not have been right for them then. This morning she could sense the love that had been shared here. Perhaps the beauty of the moments they had spent here would linger for others to breathe in as a presence, to encourage and inspire.

By the time Sara dressed, and joined Clay in the small parlor, a knock at the door announced the arrival of Joshua bringing a basket of food from the Montclair kitchen. They breakfasted in front of the fire, saying little, smiling much, eyes meeting as fingers touched in passing biscuits or marmalade.

Sara's hair, without Lizzie to dress it, fell in lustrous waves about her shoulders, and Clay noticed. "You look especially beautiful this morning, Mrs. Montrose."

The sun was well up in the sky when they finally closed the door of the little cottage and started up the road back to the big house. The snow, so deep and beautiful the day before, was already beginning to melt. And both Clay and Sara felt that in their marriage they had turned a new page that was too precious for words.

It had been crystallized in a moment the night before when they stood together at the window looking out across the snow, lighted only by stars and a ghostly crescent moon. Suddenly, across the purple darkness had flashed a shooting star — a brief streak of celestial fire almost too swift to see.

Sara had gasped and Clay had drawn her close. "A good omen!" he whispered.

Back at Montclair that afternoon, in her sitting room of the master suite, Sara unlocked the secret drawer of her small desk. With hands that trembled slightly, she drew out the packet of Theo's letters. The ribbon binding them had begun to fade, and her fingers toyed with the box. She debated whether or not to untie it, to reread them one last time.

As she hesitated, she felt a strong urge to destroy them, once and for all. In a moment of conviction, she carried them over to the fireplace and threw them, packet and all, onto the burning logs. There was a single instant of panic when she was tempted to snatch them back, but she resisted. Standing there, Sara watched the paper alight, crinkle, and curl, then vanish in a spiral of flame and smoke.

Later that same day, as she was unpacking her traveling case containing her toiletries, she drew out the Bible she had found in Leonard's desk. Unknown to anyone in the household, she had slipped it into her valise with her personal belongings just before leaving her father's home. Surely, she deserved something that had belonged to him.

Curious, she paged idly through, wondering if she would discover some other insight into his character as she and Lucie had when they found the inscription for his grave.

She turned the pages, stopping to read the underlined passages and the penciled notes in the margins. At last she paused at a verse in Philippians that had been underlined in red: "Forgetting those things which are behind and reaching forward to those things which are ahead —"

A tremor passed through Sara at those words. There was certainly more here than she was able to fully comprehend, but she thrilled to the truth she could grasp. For now, it was enough to feel that she had taken the first step out of the old, crippling bondage of the past.

Just then, from down the hall, came the sound of running feet and the high-pitched voices of little boys calling, “Mama! Mama!”

Sara turned just in time to see Malcolm rush through the door with Bryce right behind him. Her firstborn flung himself at her, clasping her around the knees, and Bryce tumbled into the arms she opened to gather both of them close.

“My darlings!” she cried, hugging them.

This was her life, here and now, in this precious moment. She would hold it fast and treasure it, Sara vowed. It was all she had, all she needed.

chapter 17

In the weeks following her return from Savannah, Sara underwent a marvelous change. It was as if she had moved from one state of existence to another. Like a butterfly emerging from the chrysalis, Sara felt a new sense of joy, and every day she felt more in harmony with her surroundings, more as if she belonged.

One morning, while dressing to visit Katherine at Cameron Hall, Sara stood in front of her dressing table mirror. Quite suddenly she seemed to be looking at another woman, someone she scarcely recognized. She leaned closer, studying her reflection critically. What was it that was so different?

Searchingly Sara stared at herself. The realization of her altered expression dawned slowly. Since that night she and Clay had spent at Eden Cottage, she had unconsciously renewed her wedding vows. Belatedly, it was true, and yet not too late, she had found love in its truest sense. With this discovery had come the assurance of Clay's lifelong commitment. She knew he would never betray her, that his was a forever love, beyond price, and that she had never fully valued it until now.

Since then, the discouraging emptiness of life had mysteriously vanished, and her restlessness and the vague hunger had disappeared. How wonderful it was to be free of all the old doubts and uncertainties that had plagued her for so long! With the exception of a few lapses, thoughts of Theo had gradually diminished.

With a smile of contentment, Sara put on her ostrich-feathered bonnet. Tying the satin ribbons under her chin, she called to Lizzie to bring her cloak, a persimmon velvet trimmed in mink, and asked her to tell Anson to bring the carriage around.

At Cameron Hall, after Sara had made the requisite visit to the nursery to admire Katherine's pride and joy, her baby daughter, Garnet, the two ladies went downstairs and settled in the cozy parlor adjoining the more formal dining room. This room, with its curved rosewood furniture covered in deep rose velvet, reflected Katherine's exquisite taste.

"Well, Sara, we haven't had a chance for a

real visit since you got back from Savannah." Kate poured tea into delicate cups and handed one to Sara. "I was so sorry to hear of your father's death. Of course, under the circumstances, I'm sure you didn't have a chance to see any of our old friends while you were there, did you?"

"A few, Kate," admitted Sara. "Mostly my father's friends who attended the memorial service." Sara hesitated. Should she mention having seen Theo? It was Katherine, of course, who had first introduced them at the Academy and he had gone to school with Doug, been in their wedding.

Even as she debated with herself, Kate leaned toward Sara and asked confidentially, "Has Clay said anything to you about the letter Uncle Logan wrote to Doug from Jamaica?"

"No. Why? Should he have?" For some reason, uneasiness stirred in the pit of Sara's stomach. She had the unsettling impression that Kate was about to tell something that would be better left unsaid.

"You know, of course, that Uncle Logan went to Jamaica to settle the affairs of a wealthy sugar planter there." Sara nodded. "Well, it seems the planter community is quite small, and everyone knows everyone else, and everyone's business, as well. Logan's client, George Campion, knew the Richardson family very well. You do remember Theo Richardson, don't you, Sara?" Kate cocked her head to one side and waited for Sara's reply.

Sara did not trust herself to speak. She merely nodded.

"Well, Theo's grandfather, Delman Richardson, was sent to Jamaica by *his* father to run the family's sugar plantation there. But the rumor was he was sent, not because he was so very capable, but to get him out of the way after he was involved in some scandal . . . no one seems to know exactly what *kind* of scandal." Kate paused and, hearing nothing from Sara, went on. "At first, this 'black sheep' son did quite well, it is said. But eventually the isolation from family, friends, all the familiar things, began to tell on him."

Sara found her tongue. "Do go on, Kate."

Kate dropped her voice lower. "He took to drinking and neglecting his responsibilities, let the overseer manage the slaves and run the plantation. Soon everything began to fall apart. The overseer was cruel, so during the slave rebellion, they murdered him!"

"Theo's grandfather?" gasped Sara.

"No, the overseer. But Logan did learn that most of the white plantation owners, at least those who were not killed during the bloody uprising, fled for their lives, taking a few loyal slaves with them when they left the island." She sat back, watching Sara's reaction.

"But, I don't understand —" Sara's puzzled frown marred the delicate perfection of her brow. "Theo was born over there, wasn't he? He told me he had lived there until *his* father came to Charleston when he was nine or ten."

"That's true, Sara. The shocking thing Logan uncovered in his investigation is that the Richardson family escaped the vengeance and bloodshed of the other planters. And the reason was —" Here Kate halted, dropping her voice to a near whisper — "that Delman Richardson, *Theo's grandfather,* was married to a *Jamaican* woman!"

When Sara did not react immediately, Kate explained, "Don't you see, Sara? Theo has *Jamaican* blood!"

Sara's hand on her teacup trembled so violently that she had to put it down.

"Of course, no one in Charleston knew or even *dreamed* such a thing," Kate continued. "Logan thinks Theo's father concealed it when they first came here. There was no trace of his background in his looks. He was quite light-skinned and very handsome, but Logan suspects that his wife, Theo's mother, learned the truth and left him because of it. Anyway, they separated. But not before they had had children — Theo and his two sisters. Incidentally, his sisters never married, so I suppose they were told. Of course, Theo and Evangeline have no children. Poor thing, her childhood injuries made it impossible for her to have any," Kate finished. "So what do you think of *that*, Sara?" she demanded and, in almost the same breath, added, "More tea?"

Sara felt numb all over. Even in her dazed state, so many things fell into place. She got to her feet.

"No thank you, Kate. I really must be going."

"Oh, must you? You've only been here such a little while," protested Kate, obviously disappointed. "I wanted to show you my new quilting pattern —"

"Another time, Kate." Already, Sara was reaching for her cape, putting on her bonnet. "I really must leave."

Sara could barely recall exchanging departing pleasantries and promises to come again soon. The next thing she knew, she was in her carriage on her way back to Montclair, her mind in a whirl.

Now so much was clear. She suspected

that Theo had found out the truth about his heritage after his father's death. The discovery had likely stunned him, and that's why he had broken off with her. To protect her! When Mr. Archer offered to settle his father's debts for the sake of the long friendship with his mother, Theo had accepted. It was all he could do to ensure the security of his mother and sisters. Then, because Evangeline was the Archers' only child, and Mr. Archer wanted a son to carry on the firm, Theo had agreed to marry Evangeline, knowing it was safe to do so since she could never bear children.

Theo had loved her, Sara, enough to sacrifice his own happiness!

She remembered his sorrowful words when she had accused him of being cruel. "Not cruel, *kind,* Sara. If we had run away and married, you might have come to hate me."

The enormity of what she had learned today stunned Sara. When she arrived back at Montclair, she went straight to her room and lay down on her bed for the rest of the afternoon.

When she finally rose to bathe and dress for dinner, she walked over to the window and looked out. The sky, just before sunset, was blue and pink and gold, like fire opals.

Soon the sun would disappear over the horizon, swallowing it in the last vestige of twilight.

How brave and unselfish Theo had been. He had given up everything so she could have all this. Her life seemed infinitely sweet to her as she gazed out at the vast sweep of lawn rolling down to the river. He had freed her for this. Silently Sara prayed for Theo, asking a gracious blessing on a man she had once loved with passionate despair, and now appreciated for his nobility of character.

chapter 18

As soon as Sara was sure she was going to have another child, she made arrangements to go to the Hydropathy Clinic in the Virginia mountains for her confinement and delivery.

The theory of hydropathy was in its infancy but Sara, always adventurous, wanted to take advantage of this revolutionary new health movement. As soon as she read about it, hailed as particularly beneficial to women, Sara was determined to avail herself of its benefits.

Based on the belief that water was the natural sustainer of life, hydropathy advocates recommended a strict regime: bathing in the natural hot springs, drinking mineral water, massage, exercise, and a vegetarian diet.

Enthusiasts claimed miraculous cures for many illnesses believed at the time to be incurable. Testimonies of all sorts of incredible recoveries were printed in the brochures sent out by the clinic to encourage women to come and see for themselves.

Sara made reservations at the most fashionable, most expensive, and best-known of the hydropathy "spas." Accompanied by Lizzie, she left Montclair in April, with Clay's somewhat reluctant blessing, three months before the expected arrival of their third child.

The mountains surrounding the resort were pink and white with blossoming dogwood against the dark green of pines, and the air was fresh and invigorating. Two large main buildings housed the dining room and kitchen, a large parlor for socializing, and a library. There was also a lounge with several writing desks, presumably for guests to use for writing to family and friends, extolling the marvels of restoration to good health they had experienced, and urging those still unconvinced to come "test the waters."

These impressive buildings faced a beautifully landscaped court with flower beds and a fountain. Behind these were the bathhouses. Paths spreading out from this center led to small, private cottages scattered among the cedar and pine trees.

Sara had reserved one of the cottages. Attended by Lizzie, she settled down to await the birth in comfort, and healthful, innovative care. This clinic catered exclusively to women, so Sara was free to walk the grounds for her twice-daily recommended exercise, stroll to the baths, and take dinner in the dining hall in the congenial company of other "patients," without self-consciousness as her date drew nearer.

"Just think, Lizzie, if I were at home, I would be a prisoner!" Sara declared to her maid. "Propriety would not allow me to go anywhere for months! I would be stifled for fresh air and sunshine."

Upon her arrival, after being shown to her cottage by one of the uniformed attendants, Sara was given a written outline of her daily schedule:

> TO OUR GUESTS, You have made the intelligent decision to take your health care seriously, and we are here to support you in that choice. We will do everything to give you the encouragement, inspiration, and information you need to derive the most benefits from your stay here.
>
> To reap the most restorative advantage from your time with us we suggest the following:
>
> 1. The hours for bathing are from 5

A.M. to 7 A.M. in the morning. An attendant will call for you. Please be punctual. No bath is to be taken in less than two hours after a meal, nor immediately after violent exercise. A rest of at least ten minutes is suggested after a walk.

2. After each bath, a glass of mineral water is to be partaken, the amount to be designated by the physician in charge of your individual treatment. Waste no time in dressing after the bath. A walk in the fresh air should follow immediately.

3. Appointments will be made for you with your physician twice a week so that you may discuss any change, symptoms, or circumstances or any other matter pertaining to your condition.

4. Hours for meals should be regularly observed, and nothing eaten between meals. In regard to diet, as in all matters, the opinion of your doctors should be strictly followed. Coffee, tea, spices, and warm or new bread are forbidden. The same in regard to tobacco or other stimulants.

5. Ten o'clock is the recommended retirement time. Read, write as little as possible, and never after supper.

Your full restoration to good health, and the assurance of receiving the total benefits from your stay, depend on you. Only those who make their health the *main object of their visit to this clinic* can expect the promised results.

This Spartan regime might have been daunting to fun-loving, luxury-prone Sara if it had not been her conviction that *this* was the way to an easier, less debilitating birth experience. In spite of its rigidity, Sara found it so much less restrictive than being under old Dr. Erling's outdated methods that she was willing to adhere to this schedule without complaint.

Besides, there were plenty of pleasurable diversions. In the evening there was entertainment for the clinic patrons, including musicales, games of charades, whist, or snap. With the strictly enforced bedtime hours everyone kept, it was a short evening anyway. With all putting in a full day of baths and exercise in the clear mountain air, most were ready for a deep, peaceful night's sleep.

Sara had never spent much time alone before coming to the clinic. Now, for the first time, she found herself thinking about her life, and wondering what the future held. On the long, solitary walks prescribed by her doctor, Sara found her thoughts turning increasingly to Clay and the children.

She realized how wrong she had been to let thoughts of Theo Richardson invade her marriage. How much they had undermined a wholehearted devotion to her husband. Regret was pointless and unhealthy, so Sara did not linger long nor dwell upon her foolish mistakes.

Although not given much to prayer, except in moments of sudden panic or desperation of one kind or another, Sara now felt an overwhelming thankfulness for her many blessings.

As Sara felt the fresh mountain air on her cheeks and breathed it into her young, healthy lungs, she felt an enormous gratitude to her Creator for so many undeserved blessings. Sara determined that after the baby came and she was back at Montclair, she would be different. She would be kinder, more thoughtful to Clay, express her love more fully. She would spend more time with the children, especially Bryce. Because Becca had taken over so much of his care, Sara's attention had been directed mostly to Malcolm. But she realized she loved both her little sons dearly, even if differently. She was overwhelmed with feeling for the new baby in a way she had not been in either of her other pregnancies.

Yes, when she went home she would change, think more about the feelings of others, not so much of herself.

In June 1842, after a short and surprisingly easy labor, Sara delivered a rosy-cheeked, eight-pound baby boy. Clay arrived a few days later and found his wife already up and about, glowing with health and happiness. They agreed to name him Leonard Leighton, and in two weeks returned to Montclair to present their third son to his brothers.

chapter 19

The new, peacock-blue velvet riding habit fit to perfection. Buttoning on the snug jacket, Sara surveyed herself in the full-length mirror. Her waist was back to its pre-baby Leighton twenty-two inches, she noted with satisfaction. But not without effort!

She tipped the velour top hat forward coquettishly, gave a final pat to the latticed blue snood that held her shiny, dark hair up from her slender neck, and touched Clay's latest gift, the new diamond stickpin fastened on the cream satin stock at her throat. Drawing on her dove-gray suede gloves, she picked up her riding crop and started out of the bedroom.

She stopped in the nursery to gaze lovingly at the rosy face of little Leonard Leighton, called "Lee," asleep in his cradle, then Sara skimmed down the winding staircase and out the front door.

Clay was standing at the head of her sleek new Arabian who pawed at the ground impatiently with his foot. Malcolm, sitting on the top step, sprang up immediately as his adored mother came out onto the porch.

Both man and boy turned worshipful eyes on the slim, elegant figure.

"You look beautiful, Mama!" Malcolm said.

Sara gave her lilting laugh, and taking his face in both hands, kissed him on both cheeks, saying, "Ah, my sweet little boy, you'll make me vain!" Then Sara ran down the steps.

"Oh, Clay, he is wonderful!" she said, patting the arched neck of the handsome animal. "Thank you, my darling, for this magnificent gift." She stroked the sleek line of the horse's shoulder. "Thank you for . . . everything!" she said, with a graceful gesture that encompassed the house, the boy, the horse. Then she placed her hand on Clay's arm lightly, smiling at him.

"Ready? Then up you go," he said, assisting her into the saddle. "Have a good ride!"

Sara lifted the reins. "I think this is the happiest day of my life!"

She threw a kiss to Malcolm, and with a flick of her crop, turned the horse. Giving a final, gay wave of one hand, she cantered down the drive. At the bend as the horse broke into a gallop heading toward the low stone fence at the end of the meadow, Sara thought to herself, *I am the happiest woman in the world.*

Family Tree

In Scotland

Brothers GAVIN and ROWAN MONTROSE, descendants of the chieftan of the Clan Graham, came to Virginia to build on an original King's Grant of two thousand acres along the James River. They began to clear, plant, and build upon it.

In 1722, GAVIN's son, KENNETH MONTROSE, brought his bride, CLAIR FRASER, from Scotland, and they settled in Williamsburg while their plantation house — "Montclair" — was being planned and built. They had three children: sons KENNETH and DUNCAN, and daughter JANET.

In England

The Barnwell Family.

GEORGE BARNWELL first married WINIFRED

AINSELY, and they had two sons: GEORGE and WILLIAM. BARNWELL later married a widow, ALICE CARY, who had a daughter, ELEANORA.

ELEANORA married NORBERT MARSH (widower with son, SIMON), and they had a daughter, NORAMARY.

In Virginia

Since the oldest son inherits, GEORGE BARNWELL's younger son, WILLIAM, came to Virginia, settled in Williamsburg, and started a shipping and importing business.

WILLIAM married ELIZABETH DEAN, and they had four daughters: WINNIE, LAURA, KATE, and SALLY. WILLIAM and ELIZABETH adopted NORAMARY when she was sent to Virginia at twelve years of age.

KENNETH MONTROSE married CLAIR FRASER. They had three children: KENNETH, JANET, and DUNCAN.

DUNCAN married NORAMARY MARSH, and they had three children: CAMERON, ROWAN, and ALAN.

CAMERON MONTROSE married LORABETH WHITAKER, and they had one son, GRAHAM. Later CAMERON married ARDEN SHERWOOD, and they remained childless.

After the death of his first wife, LUELLE HAYES, GRAHAM MONTROSE married AVRIL DUMONT. Although they had no children of their own, they adopted his nephew, CLAYBORN MONTROSE.

About the Author

Jane Peart, award-winning novelist and short story writer, grew up in North Carolina and was educated in New England. Although she now lives in northern California, her heart has remained in her native South — its people, its history, and its traditions. With more than 20 novels and 250 short stories to her credit, Jane likes to emphasize in her writing the timeless and recurring themes of family, traditional values, and a sense of place.

Ten years in the writing, the *Brides of Montclair* series is a historical, family saga of enduring beauty. In each new book, another generation comes into its own at the beautiful Montclair estate, near Williamsburg, Virginia. These compelling, dramatic stories reaffirm the importance of committed love, loyalty, courage, strength of character, and abiding faith in times of triumph and tragedy, sorrow and joy.

The employees of Thorndike Press hope you have enjoyed this Large Print book. All our Thorndike and Wheeler Large Print titles are designed for easy reading, and all our books are made to last. Other Thorndike Press Large Print books are available at your library, through selected bookstores, or directly from us.

For information about titles, please call:

(800) 223-1244

or visit our Web site at:

www.gale.com/thorndike
www.gale.com/wheeler

To share your comments, please write:

Publisher
Thorndike Press
295 Kennedy Memorial Drive
Waterville, ME 04901